AT THE TOP OF THE WORLD
AND
OTHER STORIES

AT THE TOP OF THE WORLD
AND
OTHER STORIES

by
THOMAS GRISSOM

SUNSTONE
PRESS
SANTA FE

Sunstone books may be purchased for educational, business, or sales promotional use.
For information please write: Special Markets Department, Sunstone Press,
P.O. Box 2321, Santa Fe, New Mexico 87504-2321.

Book and cover design › R. Ahl
Printed on acid-free paper

Library of Congress Cataloging-in-Publication Data

Names: Grissom, Thomas, 1940- author.
Title: At the top of the world and other stories / by Thomas Grissom.
Description: Santa Fe, New Mexico : Sunstone Press, [2020] | Includes
   reader's guide. | Summary: "These emotionally charged stories explore
   things that matter--love and honor and pity and pride and
   compassion--and speak truth to life's mysteries and perplexities"--
   Provided by publisher.
Identifiers: LCCN 2020019617 | ISBN 9781632933065 (paperback) | ISBN
   9781611395983 (epub)
Subjects: LCGFT: Short stories.
Classification: LCC PS3607.R577 A6 2020 | DDC 813/.6--dc23
LC record available at https://lccn.loc.gov/2020019617

WWW.SUNSTONEPRESS.COM
SUNSTONE PRESS / POST OFFICE BOX 2321 / SANTA FE, NM 87504-2321 /USA
(505) 988-4418 / FAX (505) 988-1025

In memory of my brother, Edgar.

CONTENTS

PREFACE

"It was making sense of things that occupied his thoughts now. It was the stories that interested him most. The ones he had lived, and the ones he had made up in his head and thought about for so long that he couldn't remember any more whether he had lived them or only made them up. Or whether he had heard them from someone else, or read them somewhere. It didn't matter, they were his now, wherever they came from.

And they were all true, as true as he knew how to make them. For him they were the only truth that mattered. Not facts. That was someone else's truth. Beyond facts. He had gotten beyond facts long ago and there was no going back. The simple facts of our existence were merely the stage on which the real truth was acted out, the truth he found in the stories by which he was able to make sense of things. Facts were never the answer to any question. Real questions had no answer. That's what made them questions. Those who insisted on sticking to the facts never seemed to understand that it is all a story anyway, and it is all true. That was the only way to make sense out of it."

A MATTER OF ENDORSEMENT

At the sound of the small brass bell above the door Andy looked up from his work. The bell made a thin musical tinkling when the opening door struck it. Mr. Ashland had hung it there so no one could come into the store unawares while he was in the back, away from the cash register up front.

By peering around and over the long shelves of stacked groceries, Andy could see an old Negro man standing just inside the door and glancing around the dimly lit store. Mr. Ashland was in the stockroom taking inventory. It was too early yet to expect many customers, even for a Saturday when most people came to town to do their shopping and take care of other business.

Mr. Ashland took care of the customers. He had been very clear about that to Andy. Andy's job each Saturday was to sweep the floors, up and down the long narrow aisles between the rows of wooden shelves lined with groceries. The floors were wooden too, and dark, almost black, from being oiled over the years to keep down the dust and preserve the wood. Andy carefully spread the oily sweeping compound, scooping up the finely-ground, sawdust-like material in a one-pound Maxwell House coffee can from its thirty-five-gallon cardboard barrel and sprinkling it evenly over the floor. Mr. Ashland had showed him exactly how much to use and how to sweep it repeatedly back and forth to work it into every little crack and crevice in the thick wood flooring before finally sweeping it all up and depositing it in the trash barrel which sat inside the door at the rear of the store. Occasionally he would check to make certain Andy was using just enough of the compound, without wasting any, and that when he had finished sweeping no residue was left on the floor.

The store smelled like fresh produce and Andy liked the

9

pleasant pungent aroma. The thick walls of the old brick building kept the interior warm in winter and cool in summer. Mr. Ashland associated coolness with darkness, and he kept the store dimly lighted in hot weather. Andy liked working by himself in the early morning in the long, dim corridors surrounded by the earthy smell of oiled floors and fresh fruit and vegetables.

Mr. Ashland had given Andy his first real job. He hired him to distribute handbills advertising items on sale in the store. He showed Andy how to place the long, thin sheets of paper on the windshields of automobiles parked along main street, slipping them unfolded behind the windshield wipers so that the writing would be easily visible to the driver; or placing them face up on the front seat if the vehicle happened to be parked with the windows open, which in the warm months of the year it most likely would be. He did not want them placed carelessly, he told Andy, where a breeze might blow them off or where they might fall out when the door was opened or fall off if the owner drove away without first removing them. Mr. Ashland believed most of all in getting his money's worth. And he wanted only one placed on each vehicle, all of which he explained to Andy several times. He paid according to how many of the printed circulars were given out. They came from the printer in bundles of one hundred fifty, and Andy was paid fifty cents for each bundle he distributed. Andy had once calculated that he received a penny for each three handbills, and for each three cars or trucks parked along the street, but that made it seem like too little money and he preferred instead to think of it as fifty cents a bundle. By going back and forth several times along main street and down each of the side streets crowded with parked vehicles he could on a good afternoon finally distribute three bundles of handbills.

Andy more than once had spotted Mr. Ashland following along discretely at a distance, checking to make sure Andy obeyed the instructions he had given him. He had hired others before Andy and let them go after discovering handbills littering the street, or creased and folded and haphazardly placed on the parked vehicles, sometimes rolled up and stuffed behind a door handle or stuck precariously in the crack of a door or window. Distributing handbills was a sporadic job since Mr. Ashland had them printed only occasionally. But he was sufficiently impressed by Andy's conscientiousness that he hired him to sweep the store each Saturday morning in advance of the heavy weekend shopping, and again when the store closed at the end of the long day.

Andy was just about to head to the stockroom to alert Mr. Ashland when he saw him suddenly appear and stride briskly and business-like toward the front of the store. He was a tall, imposing and energetic man with a stern square jaw and a blunt bald head but soft pale blue eyes. He always wore a white heavy canvas apron over dark trousers that he bought at Schoenholz's clothing store down the street, and a white shirt and thin black tie. His brown leather shoes, like him, were stern and square and sturdy. He was a deacon in the Methodist Church and had been longer than anyone else in town, and he sang in the choir each Sunday with a booming baritone voice. He and his wife lived with a daughter Andy's age in a small, modest brick house surrounded by a sprawling but tidy, well-kept lawn. His wife deferred to him in everything, and his chief interest in life outside of working seemed to be shielding his wife and daughter from the uncertainties and vicissitudes of life.

"Hello, Sam, what can we do for you this fine morning?" The booming voice filled the empty store.

"Mornin' Mr. Horace," replied the old Negro man.

Andy recognized him as Sam Baxter. Years ago he had finally relinquished any hope of making a go of it as a sharecropper on the worn-out, hard-scrabble piece of land he had tenanted for over thirty years, and he had moved from his small unshaded and dilapidated shack in the middle of a cotton field to an equally small and dilapidated house in the squalid section of town that the whites referred to as "nigger town." He took what occasional jobs he could find to support himself and his unmarried youngest daughter and her two children. He shopped at Mr. Ashland's grocery when he had money, for Mr. Ashland did not extend credit. To do so, he said, would be against the best interests of both parties; to say nothing of exposing his wife and daughter to the uncertainties and vicissitudes of life.

"Mr. Horace, you has knowed me for some time now, ain't that so?"

"For more years than probably either of us would want to admit, Sam. What's on your mind?"

"And you has always found me to be honest ain't you?"

"Well, I don't know Sam. I'm not aware of any case where you weren't. My only judge of honesty is whether a man keeps his word and pays me what he owes. You have always done that, but then I don't do business otherwise."

"You knows what I'se driving at, Mr. Horace."

"I suppose I do, Sam. I have no complaints."

11

"Yessuh, that's what I'm gettin' at."

"Does this mean that you are asking me for credit, Sam? Because if it does, I can save us both a lot of aggravation. I don't give credit to anybody. You know that as well as I do. My family's got to eat too. The grocery business ain't like it used to be, Sam. I can tell you that much for sure."

"No sir. It ain't nothin' like that, Mr. Horace. I don't needs no credit. I pays my own way or I don't go. Ain't I always?"

"You do with me, Sam, I got to agree. What is it you want then? Directly there's gonna be a swarm of shoppers in here and I'm gonna get too busy to talk."

"Only I got a favor to ask, Mr. Horace. I done some work for Mr. Will Singletary over to Ruleville—you knows him, don't you?—before I took sick and had to come on home. He mailed me a check since I wadn't there to git my cash." The old man paused and searched the store keeper's face.

"What's wrong with that, Sam? I don't know Mr. Singletary personally, but I've heard others speak of him, and I suppose his check may be good."

"Aw, yessuh, Mr. Horace. It's good all right. I knows that for sure." He paused as if collecting his thoughts. "But Mr. Nick over at the bank, he won't cash it for me. I done pleaded and pleaded with him. He says the depositors wouldn't want him to take a chance on it. But he says that if you was to endorse it, he would be willin' to cash it for me."

Nick Castleman was the president and principal owner of the First National Bank next door. Horace Ashland knew him as a hard man in a business deal, but a successful man who owed his success to hard dealing and never taking a chance where he thought there was a substantial risk of losing money. The two of them were courteous and polite but not friendly. Several years ago they had disagreed about the terms of the lease which the bank held on the building that housed Horace Ashland's grocery store. Nick Castleman had tried to raise the monthly rent as a result of several minor improvements that Mr. Ashland made to the store's interior. Horace Ashland had resisted and finally prevailed, but to do so he had to retain a lawyer and pay attorney's fees out of his own pocket. No one had been willing to take a case against the First National Bank and Nick Castleman for a contingency fee. There had been no difficulty over the lease since then, although he had made additional small improvements in the store from time to time.

Then one morning he took a sizeable deposit to the bank and received fifty dollars too much in change from the teller. He did not discover the error until he was outside the bank. He went back in and strode past the tellers' windows and directly to Nick Castleman's office in the far corner at the rear.

"Good morning, Horace. What can I do for you?" the older man asked.

"Mr. Castleman, if one of your tellers makes a mistake in a transaction and I don't catch it until after I have left the bank, will you still correct it and make it good?" he asked.

"Well, no, I'm afraid not ordinarily," he said. "You see, bank policy is that all transactions are final at the time you leave the window. That's why we always ask you to count your money. Why? What happened?"

"Good," Horace told him, "I guess I can keep the extra money your teller gave me." He left without even giving him a chance to ask how much it was. They hadn't had any occasion to speak since then.

"Let me see that check, Sam," he told the Negro man. He took it and studied it carefully. It was for a small amount.

"Why this check isn't even written on Mr. Castleman's bank, Sam." He looked inquisitively at the Negro man.

"No sir. It's on the Planter's Bank in Ruleville. Mr. Will says he has all his money in that bank."

"You need to have him give you a cashier's check, good on any bank."

"Mr. Horace, I got no way to bother Mr. Will. He's liable to think I'm accusin' him of sumpin'. And I ain't got no way to git to Ruleville 'fore I needs this money. My Janie and her children got to have things. Please, Mr. Horace, can't you help me out this one time?"

"What reason did Mr. Castleman give you for not cashing it, Sam? Did he say why, give you any reason?"

"No sir, just what I already's told you. He just says that if you was willin' to endorse it, he would make it good for me."

Horace Ashland stood for a long time as if thinking. The store had grown quiet. He turned and looked to where Andy had stopped his sweeping and was standing watching the two men and listening to the conversation. Andy quickly looked down and resumed sweeping.

"Mr. Castleman says if I endorse this check he'll cash it for you. Well, I tell you what I'm gonna do, Sam. You take this check back over to the bank and tell Mr. Castleman I said that if *he'll* endorse it,

I'll cash it for you. Then bring it on back over here and I'll give you your money." He handed the check back to Sam Baxter just as two customers came through the door.

"Yessuh, Mr. Horace," he said. "I'll sees what I can do."

The old man shuffled out the door. Andy looked up from his sweeping as the tinkling of the bell died away. He could see the stooped and bent form of Sam Baxter turn and walk off down the sidewalk in the direction opposite the bank.

A NEAT HAND

Andy stood on the corner and looked at the house across the street. Nothing much had changed in twenty-five years he thought. The modest frame house trimmed in green looked perhaps grayer and dingier than he remembered. It had seemed whiter and brighter to him back then. The raised wooden porch on the front with its low wall was just as he remembered it. On the corner behind him sat the Methodist church. Its conservative dull red brick exterior and narrow gray concrete columns stood in sharp contrast to the bright orange-red brick and imposing white columns of the Baptist church looming above it on the lot adjacent. The corner opposite the Methodist church was paved as a parking lot. Andy could recall a vacant lot there when he was growing up. He seemed to remember a used car lot also being there at one time. On the other corner a new library had been built, named in memory of an entire family that perished in a fire a few houses from where Andy had lived. He could remember the next day walking one street over to the scene and standing there staring at the burned-out house, trying to imagine what it must mean to die that way. Still, he did not know why their name had been chosen for the library.

These two intersecting streets were at the center of Andy's world when he was growing up. Court Street ran in one direction past the county court house to the center of town, and in the other to the small college where Andy had begun the long journey that was to take him far away from here. The other street led to the house where Andy lived, and the cotton fields and open countryside beyond, and in the opposite direction to the elementary school where Andy entered the first grade and the high school where he eventually graduated valedictorian. It was not, he had thought at the time, much of a distinction. There were only about a hundred students in his class and most of them expended no more effort than was necessary to merely get through and graduate. At best, he had reasoned, it meant that he was perhaps in the top ten percent. Still, there could be only one valedictorian, and he had been that one.

Andy had walked each morning along this street and past this intersection to school, and back again every afternoon. From the time he entered the first grade until he graduated from high school. In good weather he would walk home at noon for lunch—dinner they always called it; the meal one ate in the evening was supper. This intersection was the one place on his route where his mother had warned him to be careful. He had to cross the intersection at the busiest time of day, when people were on their way to and from town and the college and school and work. His mother warned him so often that eventually it became a game the two of them would play. Andy would repeat the warning aloud before his mother had time to. "I know," he would say, "be careful crossing the intersection at Court Street." He rarely left the house in the morning or at lunch without going through the ritual. When he was older and in high school it became Andy's way of gently teasing his mother whenever he thought she was being overly protective or too concerned about him. To the day she died it was their private way of communicating the bond and the understanding that existed between them. When she went to the hospital for the final time after her last stroke, he had called her on the phone. She was having trouble speaking and he simply told her, "Be careful crossing the intersection at Court Street." He knew she would understand. It was the last thing he ever had a chance to say to her.

But Andy had been careful. And he had always heeded his mother's warning. He would stand on the corner at the intersection and look both ways, left and right and in front and back of him, and wait until the cars were all clear before finally stepping off the curb into the street. He never rushed headlong across but walked calmly and deliberately. She had cautioned him about tripping and falling down in the street. On his way home from school in the afternoon he would stand on the corner beside the white house with green trim and wait patiently before crossing the intersection. It was at those times that the woman who sat in the rocking chair on the porch behind the low wall would call to him.

"Young man, young man," she would call out. "Come here, young man. Come closer so I can talk to you."

Andy would leave his place beside the curb and go dutifully

along the short concrete walk that led to the painted steps at the front of the house, and up the three steps to where he waited politely at the edge of the porch to see what she wanted. For some reason that he never understood she took a special interest in him. Out of all the school children who passed her house he was the only one she ever called over. Andy was flattered by the attention but also self-conscious and slightly awkward. He never felt he had done anything to be singled out.

She asked him his name, but she always called him "young man." Andy already knew her name. She was Mrs. Rafferty. He had heard his mother say that she was a widow who lived by herself on a small pension. Her husband was killed in a railroad accident. She had been barely middle-aged then, Andy realized now, but at the time she had seemed to him much older. Her hair was already beginning to fade from red to gray and she always wore it up on top of her head in a neat bun. She had a round face and wide gray eyes that were remarkably clear and to a young boy seemed to take in everything. She wore tiny glasses with small octagonal lenses in a gold wire frame. Her face was perpetually frozen in a pleasant expression, and her mouth seemed always on the verge of a smile. Her voice for someone so slight was deep and firm and commanding.

He stood there the first time with his school books waiting for her to speak.

"Young man, do you like school?" she asked him.

"Yes ma'am," he answered.

"What about it do you like best?" she asked.

"Reading, I suppose," Andy said.

"And are you learning to write your letters?"

'Yes, ma'am," he said.

"You must work hard and learn to write well, young man," she told him. "Nothing so much distinguishes a person of refinement as writing a neat hand. Fine penmanship is the mark of a gentleman. The most successful men I have known all wrote a beautiful hand. You take Mr. Castleman, the President of the First National Bank. Why no artist ever lived who could draw a more beautiful and perfect script. You practice your letters, young man, and learn to write a pretty hand." She smiled at Andy and brushed her hand across his hair.

"Yes ma'am," Andy answered.

He never forgot it either. They talked about other things that day and on those occasions after that when she saw him at the corner and called him over. But that was the thing that stayed with him and made such a lasting impression, her advice to learn good penmanship. She repeated it many times as a matter of great importance. Over the years he had come to associate it with the kind interest that a stranger had shown to a young boy, and the encouragement he drew from it. It was a constant memory that he carried with him from those days. Funny how a chance remark can have such an effect on a young boy, Andy thought as he stood on the corner and looked across the street at the house. It became an obligation to repay the kindness she had shown him.

He worked hard to be worthy of it too. Every day he practiced for hours, neatly printing the letters of the alphabet in his writing tablet. He went slow and did not bear down so that he could erase the imperfect attempts and try again until the pages of his tablet were filled with letters as exact as he could make them. When each tablet was full he worried his mother until she bought him a new one, and he began again. He did this with every letter of the alphabet, upper case and lower case, each one just filling the allotted space between the straight lines on the ruled pages.

At first he liked the capital letters best. More of them were symmetric about some direction, and he could use that to try and make both halves the same. There were seventeen of these, counting the K the way he made it and the Q without the little squiggly at the bottom. Some were symmetric about a vertical axis, others about a horizontal axis, and some were symmetric about both directions. Two were even symmetric about every direction. He judged the perfection of them by how closely the two halves matched when he finished writing them. Three others were not symmetric but could be divided into two pieces that had the same shape. For the six unsymmetrical ones he tried to use the same idea on each part of the letter but it was harder to do. Only ten of the lower-case letters were symmetric, and the sixteen that were not were more difficult to judge. But they were smaller than the capitals, and he could make each one more quickly and the imperfections were not as glaring. He found it easier to exactly fill the shorter half-spaces between the straight lines on the ruled paper, and he soon came to prefer the small letters. He was glad when they finally stopped printing with all capitals and began learning the rules of capitalization.

Given enough time, and with enough concentration, he could print reasonably well, but practice as long and hard as he might he never learned to print quickly with any precision. His speed exercises always came back with little notes reminding him to pay more attention to neatness.

It was the same later when they came to cursive writing. Through long hours of practice he managed to form each letter to match the ones shown in the writing manual. But when he tried to string them all together with any speed they deformed into shapes bearing only a generic resemblance to the intended result. He remembered the first time he realized that he might never be able to live up to Mrs. Rafferty's admonition to write a neat hand. He remembered too the disturbing sense of regret and disappointment he felt.

As he advanced, he tried to resurrect some small victory from defeat by reducing the size of his letters; at least that way he could write faster with some legibility; and then by reverting to tiny printed letters that were more precise and more legible; and finally to a tiny, barely legible scrawl that was a rapid combination of printed and cursive letters, by which he could write almost fast enough to keep up with his thoughts and which he at any rate could always read later. At some point he resigned himself to defeat. He had tried hard but failed. He admitted to himself what he now knew. He would never meet the goal Mrs. Rafferty had set for him. It was just not to be. At least a *small* ugly thing is better than a *big* ugly thing, he consoled himself. And over the years he had come to like his tiny almost illegible scrawl. It was fast and efficient and it served the purpose.

And Mrs. Rafferty's advice had served a purpose too he realized now. The hours he spent practicing had something to do with why he liked to write at all he suspected. She had given him a challenge and he had labored long and hard to meet it, developing good work habits and diligence and perseverance and tenacity, and he had learned to cope with his limitation and to work around it. The thoughts conveyed by the crooked lines on the page were what mattered, he had come to realize, not the tiny twisting lines themselves. And the imperfection of the forms on the page had taught him to think about the imperfection of the ideas they represented, and about the imperfection of all ideas no matter how expressed. Such a small thing, he thought; yet he knew he owed her a large debt for the interest she had shown in a small boy more than thirty-five years ago.

As he stood staring at the house and remembering, an elderly woman opened the front door and stepped out onto the porch. She walked carefully, stooped and gray-haired, to a chaise lounge and sat down. It was about the same time of day when he used to come by on his way home from school. Why, it's her, he thought. She looked much the same as he remembered her, only older and tinier and frailer. He had promised himself that if by some chance she happened to still be here he would speak to her, if only for a moment. It was part of his growing need to reconnect with the past and the people in it, as he tried to reach out and get beyond the present and face what he knew he must do in the future if he was to find any happiness.

He crossed the street and the narrow front yard and stepped up to the edge of the porch.

"Mrs. Rafferty?" he said.

She looked at him as if not actually seeing him. The gray eyes were still clear but more sunken, and the round face still pleasant enough; but the thin lips once always on the verge of a smile seemed frozen now in a kind of stiff grimace.

"Yes?" she said.

"Mrs. Rafferty, you probably don't remember me but I'm Andy Johnston. I used to live down the street when I was growing up. I've been gone from here almost twenty-five years."

"No, I can't say that I do," she replied, looking at him closely now.

"I passed here each day on my way home from school. We talked sometimes, don't you remember? You would call me over and we talked about school. That has been over thirty-five years ago."

"No," she said, "I don't seem to recall that."

"One thing you told me, I remember; that I should learn to write a neat hand. I have never forgotten that. I just wanted you to know that it made a difference. I still think about it after all these years."

"Well," she said, "I don't remember that, but I remember a lot of things from back then. I know the young people were better behaved and had more respect in those days. Lordy, sometimes I can hardly believe how bad things have gotten. It's a living shame what's happening now. It's all the niggers' fault."

She grew animated and angry. The wide gray eyes were no longer sunken, and the thin tight lips fairly snarled. Only the fine thick steel-gray hair done up in a fashionable bun on the top of her head retained any look of gentility.

"Especially the young ones. They expect everything to be handed to them on a silver platter. No respect for authority or the law or their elders. They hate anything and everything white. Yet they want everything we have without having to work for it. Well, I've got news for them. We don't want to associate with niggers either. Not now, not ever. Just let them stay in their place. I don't know what it's all coming to, where it will lead."

"I'm sorry," Andy said, "I didn't mean to upset you."

"Don't you worry yourself about me, young man. I can take care of myself. I've managed to make my own way since long before you were born, I suspect."

"I mean maybe it's just too soon," Andy said, "too early to tell yet. About how things will eventually work out, I mean."

"Oh, it's plain enough how they're working out, young man. They haven't changed. They never will. They can't change. They were all better off before."

"Well, I suppose there is resentment and misunderstanding on both sides." He made some further small attempt to reassure her.

She stared at him accusingly. "You're not one of them now, are you?"

"No ma'am," was all he could think of to say.

Andy stood in awkward silence for a few moments that seemed to him much longer. She was no longer looking at him, but beyond him towards the town, at something vague and distant and indistinct, as if swallowed up in a silent sullen reverie. He watched her for a few moments more, until he was afraid his staring would call attention to itself; then he thanked her again, apologizing for the unannounced intrusion, and made his way politely down the walk and across the street toward the church.

He looked back once briefly to see if she was looking at him, to find her still staring off into the distance. He felt sad; and shaken. I'm sorry I came, he told himself. It wouldn't have made any difference, he thought. He looked around him. I guess nothing much has changed in twenty-five years. No, that's not true, he said. A lot has changed.

THE GREAT BANK ROBBERY

The air inside the barbershop was cooler at least. Not because of air conditioning, for there was no air conditioning anywhere in town, but because an attic fan pulled in cooler air through a window beneath the shade trees that grew beside the building, and the ceiling fans rotating monotonously above each of the barber chairs kept the air moving. The air in the shop smelled of Wildroot Creme Oil and Fitch's hair tonic and Aqua Velva after-shave lotion, and the boy liked the pleasing, soothing aromas. Outside, it was one hundred degrees in the shade with an oppressive relative humidity. Tonight, like last night and every night for the past two months, the temperature would gradually cool down to the high eighties before climbing back up to a hundred or more by mid-afternoon of the next day. It was the kind of sticky, suffocating heat that wilted even a strong person by mid-morning.

It was the same climate that had made the Mississippi Delta an impenetrable jungle of cane and brier and cypress swamps before the land was cleared for the rich deep black alluvial soil that could grow cotton taller than a man's head and yield two bales of ginned lint per acre. But not this year. This year was the driest anyone could remember. Coming on the heels of the poor cotton crops from the past two summers, this year's crop could only be described as a kind of natural disaster. The plants were barely two feet tall, the foliage thin and already yellowing in scattered patches that left the fields looking like threadbare, patchwork quilts. The small hard bolls hanging green and tightly closed from the prematurely browning stalks would, when opened, yield in most places not even half a bale per acre. At thirty cents a pound that would mean a return of less than seventy-five dollars an acre for farmers who had already spent more than that just to plant and raise the crop.

It was what anyone in town talked about anymore when they roused themselves from their heat-induced torpor and bothered to talk at all. Everyone anywhere in the Delta realized by now that the prospects for this year's cotton crop were dismal, and final. It was too late. Rain now would do little to redeem the withering cotton plants anemic for too many weeks earlier in the summer when moisture might still have revived them and grown the stalks and swelled the bolls to a level even of minimal profitability. There was little need any more to talk about what was already accepted as an inevitable and foregone conclusion.

There was little need either to talk about what had been understood for generations, until, by now, everyone who grew up in the Delta to the age of the boy had assimilated into his very being, without need of articulation, the gist of that unnecessary conversation so that it became practically one's heritage and a precondition of one's existence in that peculiar landed economy. The cotton economy of the Delta was a chimera, a charade in which all acquiesced. Farmers who held the land by birthright—ceded from the time of financial ruin and social chaos after the Civil War, when momentarily the land had been actually worthless if for no other reason than it wouldn't support anyone even if the means could have been found to work it—borrowed from local banks the substantial sums of money they required, but did not themselves possess, to plant and cultivate their crops, the fortunes of which were in any given year problematic at best and at worst ruinous. Cotton farming, requiring as it did the investment of large amounts of capital, was financially precarious under the best of conditions. It only became profitable when practiced on a large scale, involving thousands of acres, along with which the potential magnitude of failure increased on the same scale. Profitability had to be measured over years, not over any single growing season. Banks loaned out this so-called "furnish" of operating capital to the farmers against the ledger value of their land as collateral, with the clear realization they wouldn't foreclose on the land even upon default of the debt in any given year. Bankers weren't in the business of growing cotton; and no one in the Delta possessed the enormous sums needed to actually pay the ledger value of thousands of acres of fertile Delta soil at auction to clear the mortgage. So bankers who may have appeared to hold title to land they neither wanted nor had any financial use for continued to provide each year's "furnish" to those farmers who were, on the average, solvent over a span of years, regardless of their misfortune in any single season. Only those planters, or those banks, which could not manage an average profitability over a sufficient span including good years and bad succumbed to this tacitly understood economic arrangement.

Bankers loaned out substantial sums of capital which farmers then spent to raise their crops, both sides appearing prosperous, even wealthy, by Delta standards, only by virtue of money that was not theirs and which if held by anyone on either side and not constantly shifted from one debt to another would have caused the entire scheme to fail like the withering stalks of this summer's cotton crop. It had been this way for generations now, ever since the disastrous calamity of the Civil War. Those who bothered to think about it at all soon understood the thin veneer of the Delta's economy for what it was. Most shrugged in resignation and saw little need to discuss, or question, what had long since become established and accepted as a way of life.

None of this much concerned the boy in any way he was conscious of on this sweltering summer day. He sat contented in the cooler air of the barbershop reading a magazine, mostly unaware of the desultory conversation of the other customers spoken in voices so low they approached the level of a murmur in his ears, punctuated by long pauses in which there seemed really nothing else that needed to be said and certainly nothing of immediate interest to him.

Over the years the barbershop had become a special place to the boy. It was here that he had been made most aware of the passage from childhood to adolescence and of the gulf that still separated him from manhood. From the time his mother deemed he was old enough for his first haircut he had been coming here, the frequency dictated in the beginning by the wishes of his mother and only later by his growing self-consciousness about his appearance. He would sit patiently in one of the wooden rundle-backed chairs lining one side and back wall of the shop, with his mother, waiting his turn. Then Mr. Beach would pump the long handle on the side of the pneumatic chair to raise it as high as it would go, and place across the arms of the chair a board on which the boy sat with his head raised to the height of the barber's spectacled gaze, his feet barely touching the cushioned leather seat. He sat very still, draped with the loose-fitting apron tied around his neck, while the locks of shorn hair cascaded noiselessly to the floor around the pedestaled base of the chair. The wall behind the barber chairs was lined with mirrors that extended to the ceiling, and he liked being the center of attention and being able to see everything in the shop when the chair was rotated at the end to let him view himself in the mirror. On the shelves beneath the mirrors stood rows of round, long-necked bottles filled with exotic smelling liquids. His earliest memory of getting his hair cut was the pleasant aroma of the cooling lotion Mr. Beach rubbed around his ears and on his neck to soothe the skin where the barber had used his straight razor to shave the hair close. The large plate glass window at the front of the shop looked out upon the enterprise and commerce of Main Street, and there was no sense of any divide between the concerns and views expressed by the conversation in the barbershop and those of the larger world outside.

Then one day Mr. Beach did not put the board in place and instead reached down and lifted the boy onto the thick cushioned seat before pumping the long-handled lever to raise the chair. Afterwards they never used the board again. At some point his mother no longer remained with him while he had his hair cut. She would sit him in one of the wooden chairs along the wall, instruct him to wait his turn and tell him to stay there until she returned for him later. Before leaving she always spoke to Mr. Beach in a voice loud enough for the boy to hear, "You let me know now if he misbehaves," knowing full well that such a public admonition assured that the boy would not. Not that the boy thought the barber would betray him, but that he thought his mother would surely know in any case if he misbehaved.

The boy recognized these changes as significant milestones in his growing up. He could recall his private satisfaction at finally being able to sit in the barber chair like everyone else. And at having the other patrons see him climb unaided into the wide expanse of the deep cushioned seat and, placing his hands on the arms of the chair, turn and seat himself while Mr. Beach worked the lever back and forth to raise the chair to the proper height. And though in the beginning it made him nervous, he liked being left to wait by himself. The only nervousness came from having to assert himself when it came his turn, and he soon got over that. He rather enjoyed the responsibility of keeping track of who had been there before him and who had come in afterward and the sense of fair play he derived from declaring and taking his turn when the time came. He felt a certain kind of pride and self-importance when he walked from his seat along the wall to climb into the barber chair, which since it was that of the proprietor, stood prominently at the front of the shop. He discovered too the magnanimous feeling of generosity that came from sometimes relinquishing his turn and deferring to someone else who had not been keeping track, or who had some special requirement or constraint to which he could defer and thereby insinuate himself even to that small extent into the adult affairs of the other customers.

The barbershop was part of the adult world. His mother at first had seemed a natural part of that world. But when she started leaving him on his own he realized that it was a man's domain and his mother seemed suddenly out of place. He lost his nervousness at being left alone and he was soon uncomfortable with her presence. Even without his mother there he realized that he too was out of place. That he was merely a boy, a child, in a man's world. With that realization the barbershop became a special place and took on new significance in his life. He began paying special attention to the things that before had only made him seem out of place. He listened to the grown-up conversation. He came to recognize the profane, and then the colloquial, from the more proper speech he was used to at home and at school. And he came to distinguish those who used profanity and poor grammar from those who did not, and he wondered what caused the difference. He didn't fully grasp much of what he heard. He was often puzzled by the laughter of the men and couldn't understand what was being implied or suggested. He took that as a matter of course and did not let it bother him. Instead he kept quiet and paid attention, even when he didn't understand and even when he pretended to be unaware of what was going on around him.

He was especially drawn to the magazines he found there. Not all of them, but some in particular. Mr. Beach subscribed to a few magazines chosen to entertain the children and the mothers who accompanied them. Those he read at first but soon lost interest in. But the other magazines were there to entertain the men. And those the boy read avidly from cover to cover for everything that he could learn about what he imagined was the grown-up world of adults.

From the time he learned to read he had been an incessant reader. His knowledge and understanding of the world were shaped much more by what he had read than by anything he had experienced. The experiences he imagined from his reading were to him every bit as real as his actual experiences. If anything, the part he pictured in his mind seemed even more real to him than what he had encountered for himself. The imagined and the real ran together and were all mixed up in his thinking until the two were no longer separate but were one and the same. He liked nothing better than to immerse himself in the imagined world conjured up by whatever he was reading. He was especially drawn to reading what was beyond his comprehension and trying to figure it out for himself. And in that way he read everything he could get his hands on.

Before taking a seat he would rummage through the magazines and choose three or four at a time, then read them as fast as he could, often skipping his turn when it came in order to finish what he was reading, sometimes staying on after he had his hair cut to finish something he had started before while waiting.

From the issues of *Field and Stream* and *Outdoor Life* and *Sports Afield* he learned about fly fishing and roll casting and the different wet and dry flies and how to fish them, how to fish wet flies across and downstream and to set the hook by feel and to fish dry flies upstream letting them drift unobstructed with the current, and how occasionally to let a dry fly sink downstream at the end of the cast to entice a reluctant fish to take it underwater when it wouldn't rise to take it on the surface. He learned about hunting deer and elk and turkey and ducks and upland game birds and which rifles were best for the one and which shotguns for the other. He learned by heart the ballistics of all the popular rifle cartridges and the patterning of each of the shotgun gauges and he had his favorite models of both long before he owned one of either, and what he had learned from reading about them shaped his choices later on. He learned the habits of all the game birds and animals and fish and every bit of the natural history and natural lore of each that he could glean from reading. He understood the concepts of natural history and conservation long before he encountered them elsewhere. Soon he could discuss these things hypothetically with others, with an apparent knowledge and wisdom that went well beyond his years and far beyond anything he had experienced for himself; though in his mind he sometimes convinced himself that he had experienced what he knew only by reading about it. He did the same with whatever topic he found in any of the magazines. He would search out that topic in the other issues and read until he felt confident about what he knew.

Those he liked best were magazines with names like *True* and *Saga* and *Adventure* that projected a kind of gritty realism. He read enthralled about shipwrecks and smuggling and modern-day pirates and about being lost at sea or stranded in the wilderness in the frozen north or the steamy jungles of the tropics. About searching for lost treasure and lost civilizations and hunting dangerous game and man-eating tigers and leopards. He suspected that much of what he read in those magazines was not actually true or was greatly exaggerated, but that didn't matter. It was still a glimpse of a world beyond the reach of his years. It opened his thinking to possibilities that he had not imagined before and to a world that even if only partially true still held out the promise of something he might someday experience but could only hint at now through the words of these, to him, anonymous, faceless writers. He had yet to formulate in his mind any clear distinction between reality and fiction and whether one was possible without the other. Trying to separate the two was not something he ever thought about.

In the pages of *Ring* magazine he read accounts of boxing and recounts of actual bouts between Ezzard Charles and Jersey Joe Walcott and Joe Louis that he had listened to on the radio with his father. He had never actually seen a boxing match, but he could picture every detail of them in his mind from the blow-by-blow descriptions on the radio, and he relived them later again and again through the written accounts in the magazines. He knew a great deal about boxing from reading about it. How to jab and feint and parry and how to punch and counterpunch, how to move his feet and upper body and how to fake with his head, how to circle to the right when jabbing against a right-handed opponent and to the left against a southpaw and to keep his gloves up to deflect blows to the head and how to keep his arms and gloves together, vertically, in front of him to cover up. He had thought about the tactics designed to get inside an opponent's punches without getting hit in order to throw a punch, and he had thought about the moves designed to counter them. He was saving his money to buy boxing gloves so that he could try it for himself and find out if he could put into practice what he had learned from reading about it. The pair he wanted was in Nielson's Mercantile and Sporting Goods store and cost ten dollars. So far he had half that amount saved.

Today was Saturday and the barbershop was crowded, as though everyone with nothing better to do had come there seeking to escape for a little while the relentless heat outside. Most of the men were farmers who because of the drought did have nothing better to do. Here at least they would not have to sit and stare at the stunted stalks standing stark and forlorn in the powdery soil of sun-parched fields, reminding them of the dwindling prospects of this year's cotton picking.

The boy had already had his haircut, but since it was Saturday he could stay and read for a while before his mother would begin to miss him at home. He was finishing an article on Schliemann's discovery of the ruins of ancient Troy. He had never read Homer or the *Iliad*, but he knew now that he would. While he sat reading, two of the men, one having his hair cut, the other seated along the wall in front of him, intruded on the background murmur with an exchange about the drought. Both were long-time farmers and each had several sections of some of the best bottomland in the entire Delta planted in cotton. Both had survived their share of lean years as well as enjoying more profitable ones.

"My God, but it's hot out there," one of the men said. "I know we've been through some bad ones before, Milton, but this has to be the worst drought I've ever seen."

"Dry out your way, is it, Shorty?" the other man replied, baiting him.

"Dry? Why those old hens of mine hadn't laid anything in months but dehydrated eggs. Won't even have to refrigerate 'em. I've been thinking lately of starting a new business seein' as how cotton farming don't pay worth a damn anymore. And nobody in the whole Delta is selling any chewing tobacco for the plain reason it's too dry to spit. Maybe I can get 'em to take my dehydrated eggs instead. At least anyway until this drought's over."

"I'll swear, those dried-up puny little plants of mine," the other man said. "I don't think the worn-out spindles on my old cotton picker even reach that low. And it would take a bunch of broke-back midgets and dwarfs to stoop over far enough to hand-pick my crop."

"Hell," the first man joined in, "from what I can see there won't be no cotton pickin', not this year, not that scrawny mess of nothin' out my way." He paused for a moment as if thinking to himself about something. "I'll tell you the truth, Milton, if it don't rain pretty darn soon, I guess I'm gonna have to rob a bank."

"Hell, Shorty," the other man replied, "if it don't rain pretty soon, we already have."

Everyone in the barbershop laughed out loud at that.

The boy laughed too, but only after hesitating a moment too long, and not out loud. As he did, he looked around to see if any of the men noticed he had laughed. He was relieved that they did not seem to notice him. Only later would he begin to realize what he was really laughing at.

By then there would be a lot of other things too he was not sure about anymore.

A FRIENDLY ENCOUNTER

"Room! Atten-hut!"

The three cadets in the long narrow dormitory room snapped to attention, staring straight ahead in the direction they were facing when the command was given. The two cadets on either side of the room stood looking toward each other, or rather past each other at some indiscernible spot on the wall, their faces frozen in a look of rigid amazement like startled animals caught in the glare of headlights. The cadet who barked the command faced the open doorway. Through the window behind him the sprawling building that housed the academy dining hall was visible across the lighted parade ground. To the right of it the gleaming glass and metal spires of the chapel rose towering in the lights like the fingers of hands clasped in prayer. Snow was falling from the blackened sky and the swirling flakes made crazy dizzying patterns in the light.

In the hallway just beyond the open doorway stood the object of the sudden attention. The color of the trim on his bathrobe identified him as a third classman. The three cadets standing at attention were fourth classmen. No one in the room spoke.

"Well, mister. Aren't you going to invite me in?"

"Yes sir. I mean, please come in, sir." The cadet facing the doorway stammered out an answer.

"That's better, mister. Only next time see that it doesn't take so long."

"Yes sir. I mean, no sir. May I ask how we can help you, sir?" He was starting to regain his composure.

"You could. And when I'm ready I'll get to that. Is that understood?"

"Yes sir."

"Good." He looked at each of the three cadets. "Why aren't

30

you studying? Don't you know it's less than an hour before lights out? You couldn't be finished with your work. Surely by now you realize that here your work is never finished?"

"Yes sir."

"I'm talking to all of you."

"Yes sir." The other two cadets sang out in unison, still staring straight ahead.

"Okay. That's more like it. You won't make it here by wasting your time. You do understand that, don't you?"

"Yes sir." The three cadets answered in unison.

"Now then. I'm looking for Cadet Andrew Johnston."

"That's me, sir," the cadet facing the doorway spoke.

"What, mister?"

"I don't understand, sir."

"What did you just say?"

"I'm sorry, sir. I mean...that is I, sir. I am Cadet Johnston, sir."

"Very well. At ease mister."

The other two cadets remained stiffly at attention.

"You two. Parade front." He gave the command without raising his voice. The two cadets pivoted to face him, still at rigid attention.

"At ease," he said, and they relaxed, still standing straight, shoulders back, but less stiffly now.

"Don't you two have somewhere you need to go? Someone you need to study with? I want to talk with Cadet Johnston in private."

"Yes sir," they answered in unison.

The two cadets lost no time in straightening their bathrobes, tying the sashes neatly in front. They picked up their books and papers and hurried out of the room, then turned and disappeared down the lighted hallway.

"What do they call you, Johnston? Your friends, I mean?"

"Andy, sir."

"Well, Andy, I'm Cadet Third Class Ben Wilson. May I call you Andy?"

"Yes sir. I mean, please do, sir."

"Those two, would you say they're friends of yours?"

"Yes sir, I suppose so. Well...no sir. Not exactly, sir. We room together."

"No matter. You learn soon enough around here who your friends are. I understand you're pretty good at physics. Do I have that right?"

31

"I don't know, sir. I guess so, sir."

"Let's drop the sir, shall we? You can just call me Ben. I have it from a very reliable source that you can help me. Physics is not my best subject, you know what I mean?"

"Take this problem." He read from a sheet of paper that he took from the pocket of his robe.

"'A train accelerates from rest at a constant rate of sixty-four feet per second per second. How fast will it be traveling at the end of one mile?'"

Andy stepped to his desk and took a clean sheet of notebook paper out of the drawer and began calculating. He entered some numbers into a hand-held calculator.

"It would be traveling approximately eight hundred twenty-two feet per second at the end of one mile," he announced.

"That's the answer I got," the other cadet said. "But that can't be."

"Why not?" Andy asked.

"Because it makes no sense, that's why. That's over five hundred miles per hour."

Andy entered some more numbers into his calculator.

"It's approximately five hundred sixty miles per hour, sir."

"Ben," the other cadet said. "What about the rest of it?" He read from the sheet of paper once more. "'How long will it take the train to travel that distance?'"

Andy wrote some more numbers on the sheet of notebook paper and entered them into the calculator.

"The answer is twelve point eight seconds," he said.

"What? Nonsense. Only twelve point eight seconds to reach a speed of five hundred sixty miles per hour and cover a distance of one mile? That's not possible."

"No," Andy said, "not in practice. The conditions stated in the problem are completely unrealistic. For one thing, the acceleration of the train is twice the acceleration due to gravity. The passengers would feel a force equal to twice their weight pushing them back against the seat. And if the wheels are not going to slip on the tracks, the force of friction would have to be twice the weight of the train. That means a coefficient of friction greater than two. Practical values, even for rough surfaces, are less than one. The numbers given in the problem are not realistic, that's all."

"Then why put them in the problem?" the other cadet asked.

"I don't know. Maybe to test your confidence and make you

think about whether you worked it correctly. Maybe because the numbers themselves are not the point of the problem. I never look at the numbers," Andy said. "I only think about the method of solution and the principles involved. Numbers are just numbers. When they turn out to be suspicious, then I check to see if I can understand why. In this case the train described in the problem is not a real train. It's someone's fantasy."

"I see," Ben said. "Could we take a look at the rest of these problems?"

"Sure," Andy said.

For the next half hour Andy checked the answers to the other problems on the sheet. For each one he selected the appropriate method of calculating the answer, wrote down the formula, substituted the numerical values given in the problem, and found the result. He double checked each calculation. He wrote out everything carefully on the sheet of paper.

"Looks like you had most of them right," Andy said. "Whoever picked the numerical values gave no thought to whether they made any practical sense. But you were working them correctly."

"Well, that's something anyway," the other cadet said. "But I was just looking up formulas in the book and plugging in numbers and wondering why they made no sense. I didn't have any idea that I was doing it right."

He put aside the problem sheet and the pages on which Andy had written out the solutions.

"Well, then, what can I do for you, Andy?"

"Nothing, I suppose, sir."

"Ben."

"Nothing, Ben. Thank you."

"How are you adjusting to this place?"

"Okay. Umm, not so well, I guess."

"What's the matter, homesick?"

"No," Andy said quickly.

"There's no shame in admitting it."

"Well, a little, I suppose. Sometimes."

"Have a girl back home?"

Not really," Andy said, "nothing like that."

"The first classmen pretty rough on you during summer training?"

"Some of them are first class jerks," Andy said.

"Not all of them."

"Some of them are though." Andy lowered his voice. "Tony Gallo, for instance."

Ben Wilson smiled at the mention of the name.

"Some of them can't handle it," he said. "Goes straight to their heads. For the really bad ones, the little shits like Gallo, it's all just an ego trip. This place turns a few of them into real pricks." He looked at Andy. "There are ways of getting back though, of getting even. Legitimate ways."

"What do you mean," Andy asked.

"At the end of my first summer I decided to box in intramurals. There are no upperclassmen in the ring. Just me and them. Everyone is equal once that bell sounds. I made a few of them pay for what I went through."

"I guess," Andy said.

"I'm good at it too, the way you are with physics. I worked hard at it. I learned all the principles and all of the methods. And I know how to apply them."

He smiled at this last thing that he said.

"The time I spent boxing made last year go by a lot faster. You have to find some way to cope. Otherwise this place will slowly grind you down. '*Illegitimi non carborundum est.*'"

"They don't really bother me," Andy said. "I can put up with a few jerks. The worst thing is never having enough time to learn what I really want to know, the way I've always been able to. Sometimes it takes me longer. But I'm willing to spend as long it takes. Here, someone is always telling me lights out, or that I have to stop whatever I'm doing now and go do something else instead. There's just never enough time."

"It's all part of the program," Ben said. "The idea is to keep you busy, so that you don't have too much time to think. You might come to the wrong conclusion, and they don't want that. They aren't training scientists or scholars here, but officers. Men accustomed to following orders as well as giving them. Every graduate who doesn't make general or at least full colonel counts as a failure of the program."

"I realize that now," Andy said. "I guess coming here may have been a mistake."

"It doesn't have to be. You have to make out of it what you can," Ben Wilson told him.

After that neither cadet spoke. Andy was still thinking about

34

what Ben had said. Finally the other cadet spoke again and broke the silence.

"Thanks again, Andy, for helping me with the physics problems. My sources were correct. I'll probably call on you again."

"Thank you," Andy said. The other cadet's praise made him feel better.

"If you ever need to talk, my door is always open. I mean it. Don't let this place get on your nerves. I could teach you to box if you'd like. Keep it in mind."

"Yes sir," Andy said.

"Carry on, mister," Ben Wilson said. He smiled and saluted, and Andy returned the salute.

"Yes sir," Andy said.

Later, after lights out, Andy had his head under the covers and was reading by flashlight. He was reading a book of poems and they were poems about pastoral scenes and the outdoors and a simpler way of life. They seemed remote and alien to the life he was living. Still he liked them very much, even if what they said seemed far away and remote since he had come here. They described a world that seemed no longer real, but illusory, that existed now only in his imagination. It was a world that he liked thinking about.

He heard footsteps approaching in the hall. The duty officer was conducting a room check. Andy turned off the light and pulled the covers down under his chin. He kept the book and flashlight hidden out of sight beneath the covers. Sometimes the duty officer would come into the room and shine his light about looking for evidence of violations. They had caught him before, reading after lights out, and he knew if he were found out again it would mean more trouble for him. After he heard the footsteps going down the hall he would read some more. In the meantime, he thought, I must remember to thank Ben Wilson.

The next day Andy went to the wing commander's office. He turned himself in for a violation of the cadet honor code. The colonel stared at him at first with disbelief, and after that with disgust.

"Do you know what you are doing, son?" he asked Andy.

"Yes sir," Andy said, standing at attention.

"I wonder," the colonel replied.

He asked Andy a number of questions. What had the violation consisted of? Andy said he had not told the truth at inspection when questioned about shining his shoes. Who had questioned him, and when? What was the inspecting officer's name? Andy told him what he could remember. Had he done it intentionally, or inadvertently? Was he absolutely certain? There would have to be an investigation and inquiry, he told Andy. He would be interviewed by an honor court of officers and upperclassmen. They would be charged with determining if an actual violation of the honor code had occurred. Andy said that he knew the rules.

That was the irony, Andy thought. The system was set up to protect anyone who unintentionally failed to tell the truth, or whose misdirected feelings of guilt made him act out of confusion. But intentionally reporting a violation of the honor code, even if, as in this case, no actual lie had been told, was a lie in itself. Reporting the violation was thus a violation of the code, for whatever reason, and Andy already knew what the eventual outcome would be. He had thought it through carefully.

On the long ride home Andy paid little attention to the scenery out the window. The mountains rising blue and silver above the plains, with their snow-covered peaks and the sharp outlines of a woman lying on her back, were behind him. Behind that were other peaks, some as high as the ones he was leaving, and beyond that he knew there were mountain ranges and basins and deserts stretching all the way to the ocean. The prairie country ahead of him with its vastness and the tiny houses and clumps of trees that dotted it faded into the distance on either side of the bus. Compared to the mountains and the desert with its sculptured plateaus he found the prairie monotonous and depressing. He looked at it without really seeing it. He read the few books he had brought with him, and sat and thought.

He knew he would come back someday. This was where he wanted to be. He loved this country with its mountains and deserts and with its openness and vastness and emptiness between towns that made it seem empty even when there were people in it. But first he would have to go back and start over. He had a lot of catching up to do and he knew he would have to work hard. He didn't feel any true shame or disgrace. It was their system not his. He didn't care one way or the other about the principles behind it or what they stood for. He had used it for what he knew he had to do, and he did not feel any shame about that. The training and hazing and harassment he had gone through had prepared him to deal with what anyone else might think. He had no time for that anyway. He had work to do. He had lost his scholarships to Davidson and the University, and he would have to work to pay his way. He could attend college in his home town for now. He would start with that and go on from there. He would have to work very hard to catch up, to get where he wanted to be. It would be good for him.

I never did get a chance to thank Ben Wilson, he thought.

SOPHIE'S SURPRISE

Sophie woke up suddenly. Quickly she slipped out of bed and stretched for one brief moment in the warm sunshine already streaming in through the bedroom windows. She paused just long enough to brush her long brown hair and pull it back into a tight ponytail, then hurriedly dressed.

Sophie woke this same way every morning. One minute she would be sound asleep, and the next she was wide awake and leaping out of bed, hurrying to get dressed as if she had not an instant to lose. For Sophie life was an adventure. Each day held such exciting possibilities that she could not bear to waste even one unnecessary moment lying in bed. She was afraid she might miss something—something that she would be very sorry indeed to have missed. Something truly exciting could happen and she would not be there to see it.

It is true that on some winter mornings, when the bare wooden floor felt cold as ice and a thick layer of white frost coated her bedroom windows, she would snuggle down deeper under the warm covers and lie there for a minute or two after she awoke. Sophie considered such moments magical. On those mornings she wanted to hold on to that special feeling of being safe and snug in her warm bed while outside all was freezing and covered with ice. Life was not only an adventure, but one filled with wonderful moments of magic and mystery.

On this morning, however, Sophie did not linger in bed. She hastened to get dressed and downstairs to where she knew her mother would be preparing breakfast. This morning was not cold and wintry, but warm and sunny. Today marked the beginning of summer vacation and Sophie had so much she wanted to see and do. For months now school and things associated with it had kept her busy. At long last school was out for the summer and Sophie had a lot of catching up to do.

She tripped down the stairs and into the bright cheery kitchen filled with delicious smells. Strips of bacon sizzled in a pan on the stove. A plate of hot biscuits sat on the open door of the big black oven, kept warm there. Her mother was at the stove frying eggs and cooking oatmeal. The oatmeal made little plopping sounds as it bubbled up, and the eggs splattered and crackled in the skillet. Sophie had arrived just in time. It was her special job each morning to set the table.

Would you please set the table, Sophie, her mother said to her as she came through the door, though they both knew there was no need to ask. Sophie understood that it was her responsibility to set the table for breakfast. She had to hurry down in time to have the plates and bowls, and cups and saucers, and glasses for the orange juice and milk, and the knives and forks and spoons all neatly put in their proper places on the table before her mother finished cooking the breakfast. Everything had to be ready by the time breakfast was served. Sophie knew her mother was depending on her. So there was no need for her mother to say, as she did every morning, Sophie, would you please set the table, since they both realized that Sophie understood what was expected of her.

But Sophie liked to be asked anyway. It made her feel grown-up and important to have her mother ask for Sophie's help. It was like a little game the two of them played. Her mother always asked and Sophie in turn always helped. Sophie looked forward to it each morning. There was a kind of magic too in those things you could always count on, and in feeling grown-up and important.

Sophie was already seated in her chair by the time her father came to the table. All during breakfast she was eager to be finished. Don't eat so fast, her father told her. Slow down and enjoy your food.

Her parents looked forward to meal times, especially breakfast. Breakfast marked the real beginning of the day. Her mother and father would use that time to talk and make plans for what each would be doing that day. They would often include Sophie in those plans. Sometimes there would be extra chores for her to do, beyond the usual ones she did every day like making her own bed and picking up her things and putting them away. But not this morning. Today was special. This was the first day of summer vacation and Sophie would not have extra chores. She would be free to do whatever she liked, so long as it didn't break any rules.

There were always rules to be obeyed, Sophie had discovered. Grown-ups had so many rules it seemed, that at times Sophie felt overwhelmed by them. Sometimes all the rules she had to obey took the magic and the mystery out of life, she thought. Rules are important, and necessary, her parents told her.

Her teachers at school and at Sunday school taught her the same thing. Rules make the world a safe and orderly place, they said. Without rules people would not know how to behave or what was expected of them. They would not know what to do when they had to make choices, like what time to go to school or whether to cross the street. Children would not be safe from danger. Cars would run red lights and stop signs or even drive on the wrong side of the road and have collisions.

Sophie knew all the reasons. She had heard them all before. And she understood them too, as well as she could. It's just that she didn't always like having so many rules.

Grown-ups also had to obey rules. Her father had to go to work each morning at eight and he came home again at five. Sophie's mother also worked. In return they earned money to buy those things the family needed, like food and clothes. They didn't have to work on weekends, or holidays, or during vacation. There were rules about such things. Then they were free to do whatever they wished as long as they didn't break any other rules. There were always rules to be obeyed, Sophie had found.

Even with rules things could still go wrong. Not everyone followed the rules. Some people broke the rules deliberately, Sophie had discovered. Sometimes the rules were broken because they seemed unfair or because they seemed to make no sense. Sophie understood that too. At times she felt the same way. Some rules were okay, she guessed, but too many rules took all the fun out of everything.

Besides, sometimes rules didn't apply. You couldn't make a rule about whether it was going to rain and spoil a picnic, or whether you might wake up one morning and find that it had snowed while you were asleep and turned the world into a beautiful white wonderland, or whether you might suddenly meet someone and make a new friend, or about any of the other little surprises that made life so exciting. Such things were not covered by any rules — that's what made them surprises. They were a kind of magic that the world held in spite of all the rules, and it was the unexpected magic and mystery of things that Sophie liked best of all.

What are you going to do today, Sophie? her father asked. She was almost finished with her breakfast and Sophie was beginning to squirm and fidget in her chair, anxious to be through so that she could go outside and play.

I think I'll go exploring today, Sophie said. I'll go through the pasture and down to the pond, and I may even take a walk through the woods — to see what I can see, she added.

Do your chores first, her father said, and don't stay gone too long. Your mother may want your help while I'm at work. And don't forget, he told Sophie, you may go only as far as our fence by yourself. Don't go any farther than that.

That was one of the rules, Sophie knew. She had to stay inside the fence that went around the pasture and the pond and through the woods to mark the boundary where their property joined that of their neighbors. She was allowed to go anywhere she wished on her own so long as she stayed on her side of the fence.

Sophie helped her mother carry the breakfast dishes to the sink. Then she scurried up the stairs to her room. She picked up her pajamas, folded them neatly into a tidy little bundle, and tucked them away in one corner of her dresser drawer. That was the place where she always kept them. She put them there each morning. And each night, even in the dark if need be, she could always find them again without even having to look. Next she smoothed the sheets on her bed and pulled the light wool blanket up over them. She put the two fluffy pillows side by side at the base of the headboard and spread the blue and white checked cover over the bed and the pillows, pausing to smooth the wrinkles from the bedspread and tuck it neatly under the front edge of each pillow. Then Sophie brushed her teeth, and just for good measure combed and brushed her long brown hair once more. At last she was ready to go outside.

Don't forget, Sophie's father told her as he was leaving for work, Uncle Arthur is coming tonight.

Sophie didn't remember. She had forgotten all about this being the day Uncle Arthur was coming for a visit. She was glad she had forgotten. Uncle Arthur was Sophie's favorite uncle, and this way his visit was a surprise all over again. Sophie liked surprises best of all; now she had a new surprise to look forward to all day.

Sophie did not mind the rule about not crossing the fence. There was plenty to see and do on her side of the fence. She never ran out of something to explore.

Sophie liked her side of the fence best anyway. Her father

owned one of the last farms left in the valley. There were other valleys and other farms, but beyond the fence which marked the edge of their property they were beginning to be hemmed in by an ever-growing number of new streets and the new houses which sat along them. Land was becoming more and more scarce. She had heard her father and mother and the other adults talking about it. She had heard it also being discussed on TV. Sophie knew that she was not the only one concerned.

For the last two years she had watched the new houses springing up beside the road that took her to school. She found it amazing how fast the workers could build a whole field of houses where just a short while ago there had been pastures and trees and creeks and ponds, where Sophie had gone hiking or ridden her bike with her father. At the beginning of one summer there had been no houses in one of Sophie's favorite meadows where wild clover and blue thistles grew. By the time school opened in the fall the meadow was filled with houses and the houses were filled with people.

At first Sophie had not minded. She would have lots of new friends, she thought. There would be more children her own age to play with. But if they kept coming, Sophie wondered, where would they all find room to play? Soon all of the good places would be filled with more and more houses and there would be nowhere left for the kinds of things that Sophie liked to do. She did not want to have to play indoors. Sophie quickly tired of staying in the house. She liked to read at night and occasionally she did not mind being indoors with her toys; but she wanted most of all to be out of doors, exploring and seeing what she could see.

That was why Uncle Arthur was her favorite. Uncle Arthur was her mother's older brother. He was tall and kind, and Sophie thought he was very handsome with his smooth bald head and dark trim beard that outlined his face. Whenever he visited, he and Sophie would spend hours roaming about the countryside exploring each new creek and thicket they could find, while Uncle Arthur showed Sophie all the wonderful things he had learned when he was growing up. Uncle Arthur was a scientist and he knew a lot about the out-of-doors, about trees and flowers, and birds too, and about the animals and even the insects that lived in the pasture and the woods. Sophie never tired of asking him questions, the kinds of questions that she never seemed to know how to answer herself but which Uncle Arthur did.

Sophie liked being able to ask questions and she always liked

42

hearing Uncle Arthur's answers and thinking about the strange and wonderful things he told her. But sometimes it dismayed her whenever he immediately knew the answer to some new question that she had just thought of. Sophie didn't want everything to be known, and at times it seemed to her that Uncle Arthur knew just about everything.

If everything is known, Sophie thought, then soon there would be no more surprises. And no more mysteries either, and to Sophie that would have meant the end of a special kind of magic that came from believing that some things were mysterious because there were no answers. Some things must just happen, Sophie believed, for no reason at all other than they just happen. Otherwise how could one ever be surprised, or have anything to look forward to?

Grown-ups know too much, Sophie feared. There might be nothing left for her to discover, nothing new for her to learn for herself, and that troubled Sophie and made her feel sad and disappointed.

Grown-ups were able to do too much too. That was why they could build roads and curbs and streets in the pastures she used to explore, and build a whole field of houses in a single summer and find people enough to fill them up before school began in the fall. And then build the new stores and supermarkets needed to sell furniture and clothes and groceries to all those people living in the new houses, and service stations to provide gasoline for the cars that now drove along the one road leading from town to her father's farm, which Sophie could remember driving alone in the past whenever her family went anywhere. She supposed that they would just keep on until they had filled up the entire valley.

She hadn't made any new friends either. The people in the new houses kept pretty much to themselves. The children played in their own yards or attended activities at school or church in town. None of them, it seemed, were interested in exploring the fields and woods that bordered the new neighborhoods along the road. The fields had been cleared and the trees cut down to make way for the new streets and houses. Now the people who had moved in were busy pulling up the remaining wild flowers and the weeds and brambles that grew around the edges of the yards and along the ditch banks bordering the cleared spaces. In their place they planted neat lawns and small spindly trees that would take years to grow as big as the ones they had cut down.

To Sophie none of it made much sense. It was, she decided, just another mystery, and in that at least she found some solace. But for now she was too busy to worry about it. There was so much for her to see and do on her own side of the fence.

She climbed through the old wooden gate that led to the pasture. Sophie could still see the pathways through the pasture that she made last summer, though they were overgrown now with new grass and the tall rye that grew even under the snow during the winter. She got down on her hands and knees and searched until she found the tiny trails made by mice through the matted grass. At the end of one she found a mound in the tangled grass that she recognized as a nest. That was where the mice lived. They lived there even during the winter underneath the snow and used these trails to move about and find the seeds and plants that they needed for food. The mice breathed the air trapped in the snow, Uncle Arthur told her. And the snow kept them warm by insulating them from the colder air when the outside temperatures plummeted far below freezing. That way they could survive all winter beneath the thick blanket of snow that covered the pasture from late fall until it finally melted in the spring.

On her hands and knees Sophie followed a still bigger trail through the thick grass, parting the long stems carefully with her hands to trace where it burrowed through the jumbled tufts of tall grass. Soon she came to a neat round hole in the ground and not far away she found another, and then a third. That was where a short-tailed weasel—also called an ermine, Uncle Arthur told her—had lived during the winter. The weasel survived by hunting the mice, killing and eating them for its food. The ermine was all white in winter, except for its eyes and the end of its nose and tip of its tail which were black. Unlike the mice, it often burrowed up through the snow and ran about on the surface, leaving tiny tracks which Sophie sometimes saw in the smooth snow.

Now, in summer, the weasel would be brown again, except underneath where it remained white year-round. It changed its color to match its surroundings, Uncle Arthur told her, white to match the snow in winter and brown again like the dried grass and bare earth in summer. That made the weasel harder to see, he explained. Sophie did not understand how the weasel was able to change its color. That still seemed like a great mystery to her, although perhaps Uncle Arthur knew the answer to that too. She must remember to ask him. Perhaps, she thought, it was enough to know why it happened. Knowing that much made it seem less mysterious to Sophie. That explained too why the weasel always had more than one entrance to its burrow, for there were other creatures, like the mink, that preyed on weasels.

Everything must eat something and is in turn eaten by something else, Uncle Arthur had told her. With that one revelation a lot of what had once seemed mysterious to Sophie was now understandable.

Now when she thought of earthworms she thought also of the robins that ate them. Often she had watched as a big fat robin hopped about, then stopped and stood with its head cocked as if listening and looking for something that to Sophie was invisible, before hopping once more briefly and then plunging its long thin beak into the ground and plucking an earthworm from beneath the surface.

Earthworms had to eat too. They eat vegetable matter in the soil, Uncle Arthur told her. There were earthworms in the compost that her father kept for his garden. They ate the grass clippings and leaves which her father threw on the compost pile, and in turn the earthworms excreted the rich black humus which he took from the compost bin and spread on the garden each spring. Still smaller creatures, called nematodes, lived in the soil composed of the earthworm droppings. And larger creatures, like the Cooper's hawk that lived in the woods at the edge of the pasture, ate the robins.

Sophie didn't know whether anything still bigger ate Cooper's hawks, or whether there were creatures in the soil smaller even than the nematodes, which they in turn ate. It became very complicated, and at some point it had to stop, she guessed. It had to stop whenever one reached the very largest creature and the very smallest, Sophie thought.

She tried to think of something larger which might eat the Cooper's hawk, but all she could think of was the dead Cooper's hawk being eaten by ants, the way she had observed ants eating dead birds before. But that would be something smaller eating something larger, she thought. Perhaps there were bigger hawks that ate the smaller Cooper's hawks. But what ate them, Sophie wondered?

She tried to think of the largest creatures she could—horses and cows, then giraffes and elephants, even whales, kept coming to mind—but none of them ate Cooper's hawks so far as she knew, and even if they did there would be nothing bigger to eat them and it would still have to stop somewhere.

She could easily imagine creatures bigger even than whales

and elephants—like the dinosaurs whose bones she had seen once in the museum but none of them existed anymore. That was a bit of a mystery too, she decided.

It was harder for her to try and imagine smaller and smaller creatures. Once Uncle Arthur had let her look at water from the pond through his microscope. What had looked like only muddy water to Sophie when she saw Uncle Arthur take it from the pond had been full of little creatures which could be seen swimming about when she looked through the microscope.

But Sophie still had trouble imagining things too small to be seen. And what about things that might be too big to be seen, she wondered. Was that possible? Could there be something out there in the night sky where she saw nothing at all? Maybe that's where the real mystery lies, Sophie thought—in things too big and too small to be seen. Sophie liked that idea. She would ask Uncle Arthur when he came.

Sophie spent the afternoon looking for meadowlark nests in the corner of the pasture where they had nested last summer. Over and over she flushed meadowlarks from the lush dense grass but she found no nests. She had found them on other occasions. A shallow depression in the ground lined and covered with a dome of woven grass inside of which would be several white eggs streaked with browns and purples. But Sophie didn't mind. If she could find the nests so could the cats, she reasoned, and she didn't want that to happen.

So she gave up looking for bird nests and sat for a while listening to the thrushes singing in the woods. To Sophie they sounded exactly like someone playing a magic flute. Uncle Arthur had taught her to distinguish between the song of a Swainson's thrush, whose flute-like notes rose in pitch, and that of a hermit thrush, which went up and down the scale. The ones she heard now were Swainson's thrushes. They returned each spring at the same time, from South America where they spent the winter, Uncle Arthur had told her. They were shy and secretive and Sophie rarely saw one, although she could easily entice them to the edge of the woods by simply whistling the short pure note that was part of their call.

Bird migrations were another mystery. How they knew when to set out and how they found their way across oceans and through the darkness were things that still puzzled Sophie, even after Uncle Arthur had tried to explain it. It was truly a mystery that the thrushes could ever make their way back here to her father's woods from somewhere thousands of miles away. It was one of those things so surprising that it would seem no less surprising even if it could be explained in some way she could understand. She was not even sure that she could imagine what it was for something to be thousands of miles away.

Faced with her new mystery, however, Sophie soon forgot about the question of how the weasel could turn white or how the birds migrated. She kept thinking instead about things that were too large or too small to be seen.

That evening, as they sat on the porch and looked up at the stars, she asked Uncle Arthur about it. Is there anything up there where we see nothing, she asked?

That's a very good question, Sophie, Uncle Arthur said. Uncle Arthur was always pleased whenever Sophie asked him questions.

He thought for some time before answering. The truth is, no one knows, he told her. What he said next was even more surprising.

We can't even be certain that those stars we see are still there, he told her. What we are seeing when we look at the night sky is the light that left those stars many years ago, in most cases thousands of years before now. It has taken the light that long just to reach our eyes across the vast distances that lie between us and the stars. What has happened to those stars in the meantime we will not be able to see for thousands of years more. If even the nearest star were to suddenly disappear we would not know about it for more than three years. It would take that long for the news to reach us at the speed of light, Uncle Arthur said. For any of the others it would take even longer.

But I don't understand, Sophie exclaimed. Whenever I flip on the light switch at night or shine a flashlight across the pasture in the dark it seems to take no time at all for the light to reach whatever I shine it on.

It only seems so, Uncle Arthur said, because the distance that the light must travel to fill the room or to reach the pond across the pasture is so short. But our world is much larger and some things in it are so far apart that it takes a long time indeed for light to travel between them. Parts of our world may even be so big, and things in it so far away, that we can never hope to see them at all or know anything about them.

After all, we live only a short while, he went on. During that time we can only see what happens in that part of our world from which light has time to reach us while we are still here to observe it.

For everything beyond that, we see only what happened in the past, before we lived.

But isn't there anything that can go faster than light? Sophie asked. She didn't know for sure even what she meant but she was thinking of the problem that Uncle Arthur had brought up, about how long it took for light to travel great distances, and so she asked anyway.

It seems not, Uncle Arthur said.

Why not? Sophie wanted to know. Is there a reason?

I could give you some reasons, Uncle Arthur said, but I'm afraid you wouldn't be able to understand them yet, and they aren't really reasons anyway. They're just different ways of saying the same thing over again—that nothing travels faster than light. There is no reason I know of, beyond saying that. It just seems to be the way our world is, he told her. I suppose it is one of the great mysteries of the world.

Sophie sat thinking about all that Uncle Arthur had said. So there are things too big—or rather too far away—to be seen after all. She could not imagine what they must be like, but then she supposed that was just the point. She had even more difficulty trying to imagine those things that were too small to be seen.

Can we ever know what is smaller than the smallest thing we can see, she asked after a while? Uncle Arthur looked at Sophie. The look on his face seemed to say that he had known ahead of time what she was going to ask. Again he thought a long time before answering.

Yes, he said finally. Yes, and no. He seemed intent upon giving Sophie a serious answer to her question.

There are rules that determine how our world works, he told her. Just as you have to behave in a certain way according to the rules laid down by your mother and father or those at school, just as you have to live by those rules there are also certain rules which govern how the world and everything in it must behave. That rule about the speed of light is one of them. No one knows why, it just seems to be the case that nothing travels faster than light. It is one of the fundamental rules that describe how our world works, he said. There are a number of such rules, he told Sophie. We call these rules the laws of nature.

Uncle Arthur gave Sophie a few moments to think about what he had said. When he saw that she had no questions, he continued.

Well, the rules that govern things too small for us to see are very strange indeed, Uncle Arthur continued. Again, no one knows why it should be so, but the rules limit how much we are allowed to know about very tiny things. It makes no difference whether we know what those invisible things are made of or not. All that matters is that they are very small, too small to be seen even through the most powerful microscope anyone could ever make.

The knowledge we are allowed to have about such small things is of a particular kind, and it is limited, he said. In the case of these invisible bits of matter, for example, we are not allowed to know exactly where they are. Or rather, if we know precisely where they are then we can know nothing at all about how fast or in what direction they are moving. So that even if we know where they are at this instant, we will not know where to find them a moment later, he said.

On the other hand, if we insist on knowing how fast and in what direction they are moving, then we can know nothing at all about where they are located. And if we try to find out both things at the same time—that is, where these invisible bits of matter are located and how they are moving—then our knowledge of both will always be uncertain by a particular amount specified by the rules that govern such small things. He paused to give Sophie time to think about what he had said.

All of this makes the unseen portion of our world a very bizarre place, he went on. You would probably find it strange if someone asked your whereabouts and your mother said that you may be out here on the porch talking to me, and you may be at school, and you may be somewhere else. You would insist, I am sure, that you can only be in one place at a time. But the best we can do for those invisible bits of matter is to say that they may be here, and they may be over there, and they may be somewhere else. And—he said this slowly so that Sophie would have time to think about it carefully—they may be in all of those places at the same time.

You can begin to see, he told Sophie with a twinkle in his eye, what it means for things to be too small for us to see them and just what a mysterious place this unseen part of our world is.

After that Uncle Arthur fell silent and sat without talking, thinking again about the way he had chosen to try and answer Sophie's questions.

He wasn't at all sure how much of what he had told her she was able to understand. But for now, he decided, that was enough. If he tried to explain more he might only confuse her further. Better to let her think for a while about what he had said, then try again later after she had a chance to think of more questions on her own. Besides, Uncle Arthur thought to himself, Sophie is a very bright little girl.

Sophie sat quietly, thinking about what Uncle Arthur had said. What a great mystery, she thought. She couldn't imagine why the world of things-too-small-to-be-seen would obey such strange sounding rules, or why there should be that other rule about the speed of light. But Uncle Arthur had said it and it must be so, Sophie thought. Sophie always trusted what Uncle Arthur told her, even when at first it seemed confusing.

Why had she never suspected that such strange and mysterious things could be so, Sophie wondered? It was just because they involved things that were too big or too small to be seen, she told herself. How could you suspect anything at all about things you had never even seen? And yet she wondered just this afternoon if there might not be some new mystery associated with very big and very small things, and she had been right. She was glad now that she had thought of it and asked Uncle Arthur about it.

Sophie still had lots of questions. She wasn't sure which of her questions made sense. A lot of what Uncle Arthur had told her was very confusing. She would have to think about it for a long time and get him to tell her again. But she did have one thing more she wanted to ask.

What about the world we can see, Sophie asked, the world of the pasture and the pond and the woods? What do the rules say about what we can know about those things, she asked?

Uncle Arthur looked at Sophie again and smiled. The look on his face this time showed just how pleased and proud he was that she had thought of this particular question. Uncle Arthur knew how much Sophie loved surprises. He thought hard before he said anything.

For a long time the rules that govern this other part of the world seemed pretty simple, he told her. With the exception of those things that are very big or very small, it seemed that we could know as much as we wanted to about our world, and that if we knew enough we would be able to predict exactly what was going to happen, things like the weather, whether it will snow and when and how much, that sort of thing.

But the rules, it turns out, are really not that simple after all, he said. Now it seems that no matter how much we know beforehand some things will always remain unpredictable. The weather is one of them. How many mice or rabbits there will be in the pasture, and whether there will be any frogs in the pond, and how many, may be other examples. Eventually we may find that the world is far more unpredictable and full of surprises than we thought.

Uncle Arthur didn't say anything more for a while. Sophie was still thinking about this answer to her last question when he spoke again.

Young lady, it is way past your bedtime, and I think we can safely predict that your mother is going to be very unhappy if you don't scoot up to bed.

Sophie was allowed to stay up later whenever Uncle Arthur visited, but she knew that he was right and she did as he suggested. Besides, she had lots of new things to think about lying in her bed in the dark before she fell asleep. It had been a long day and she was tired, but it had been a wonderful day too, and she was already looking forward to tomorrow when she and Uncle Arthur would go down to the pond and try to determine how many frogs had managed to survive the winter buried in the mud underneath the ice.

A day so filled with surprises was the kind of day Sophie liked best of all. There had even been surprises about surprises. The rules that Sophie had encountered before were always intended to make things happen the way they were supposed to. It was nice to know there could be rules that kept one from knowing what was going to happen. That was the nicest surprise of all, Sophie thought.

Grown-ups didn't know so much after all it seemed. Some of them like Uncle Arthur knew a lot, Sophie thought, but now there were rules which kept them from knowing too much. Maybe those same rules would also keep them from being able to do too much, she thought. She must remember to ask Uncle Arthur tomorrow.

THE DOGWOOD INVITATIONAL

This is something that happened a long time ago but even so I've never been able to forget it. I remember that it seemed almost incredible at the time, and it still seems so now, but it has stuck with me nevertheless. I'm not going to try to say whether it's actually true or not, not after this many years, but the people in it are real people or at least some of them are. The others are not so unlike real people as to make it unbelievable on that account alone. Still, I suppose I wonder sometimes whether it really could have happened or not.

It was the weekend of the Dogwood Invitational, held each spring when the dogwoods are blooming in the forests of east Tennessee. The petals of the dogwood blossom form a cross. Faint brown stains, like those of dried blood from nail-pierced hands and feet or from a bleeding head crowned with thorns, anoint the curled tip of each delicate petal. Locally it is known as the Easter flower, and on a good year it is blooming by then. This was back before the discovery of the devastating blight that is killing off native dogwood trees all across their eastern range; long before anyone had noticed the trees beginning to sicken and die, shedding withered brown and gray leaves from the tips of dry brittle branches. In those days no one had even heard of the disease. Each spring the delicate petals dotted the woods, like pink and white butterflies flitting among clumps of redbud blossoms or floating beside creamy white racemes dangling from the delicately drooping branches of sourwood trees. Then archers from all over Appalachia and beyond flocked to Knoxville for two days of tournament shooting, on a picturesque course that wound up hill and down through blossoming dogwoods in a dense southern forest of sweetgum and pine and hickory and oak.

The Dogwood Invitational attracted some of the best archers in the region and more than one of these shooters went on to win national championships. The level of competition was unsurpassed. That's what brought them from all over, to test themselves against the best shooters around. You can find some of their names in the record books still. You won't however find the name of the preacher recorded there, for the simple reason that he shot only the first day of the tournament. The second day of course was Easter, and the preacher had a small country church with a congregation to tend.

In the beginning, archery had been a simple affair. But by then it was becoming a grimmer, more serious business. At first a tournament was just a convenient excuse to get together with a group of friends and have fun, to practice for hunting season or to show off new equipment and swap stories. A field range was laid out to simulate the kind of conditions encountered in hunting. The terrain was uneven, the distances were unmarked, and everyone shot pretty much the same type of equipment. Each archer was recognized and esteemed for his individual idiosyncrasies of style, equally for his characteristic shortcomings and failings as much as for his prowess or successes. Each shot was a separate adventure, just as in hunting. Then, inevitably, someone began keeping score.

Instead of being satisfied with those individual instances when a shot was well executed and the shaft flew, unerring, to its mark, archers began seeking assurance in numbers. Numbers that reflected not how well the first shot, or an occasional shot, was made, the way success in hunting is measured, but how consistently one could shoot whole groups of arrows. Scores made the game unrelenting and brutally objective. No longer could a shooter rationalize those arrows that missed by pointing to the spectacular hits. The failures refused to go away. They stood there, implacable and undeniable in the leering numerical columns of the total score, visible to all in the final diminutive magnitude of a single number. The fun of the moment became lost in the labors of a day; whole careers could be summarized in a few bleak rows of sterile ciphers.

The competition for higher scores became relentless. Suddenly anyone who knew the exact distance to the target possessed an advantage. To prevent cheating and give everyone an equal chance, the yardage was posted on the shooting stakes at each target. Once the distances were known it was a simple matter to affix an adjustable sight to the bow, calibrated for each of the prescribed distances. With that the guesswork was taken out of aiming. One simply held the sight pin in the center of the bullseye to choose the elevation and windage that sent the arrow along the correct trajectory.

From calibrated sights it was but a short step to other paraphernalia designed to further take the guesswork out of shooting. Apertures, or peep sights, mounted in the string; bubble levels on the bow to indicate when it is vertical; mirrors, clickers, and other gadgets to assure that the arrow is drawn precisely the same distance on every shot; weights and rods screwed into the bow to stabilize it; hand-held devices with which the string is drawn and then released mechanically by squeezing a trigger or pushing a button. The possibilities are limited only by the imagination and human ingenuity.

Soon there had to be separate categories of shooters. The freestyle shooters allowed the use of all the latest technological trinkets. The traditionalists banned them all outright. In between, there were numerous other categories, each of which allowed certain innovations while prohibiting others. Members of the different groups eyed each other suspiciously across their equipment, as if the whole point of the sport was to figure out a cleverer way to cheat in order to gain some slight advantage leading to a higher score.

Yet who could quarrel with success? The gadgeteers turned in higher scores than the traditionalists, though it would be foolish to be dogmatic about it. The result was a triumph for technology. The traditionalists complained that something vital was being lost, but frankly none of them seemed to be able to say what it was. You might as well mount the arrow in the barrel of a rifle, they scorned, and propel it on its way with gunpowder, and be done with it. Then it wouldn't have to be so long, or need feathers, and it would fly faster and farther and be easier to aim. But at this point in the argument no one was still listening. Such was the backdrop against which the events of the Dogwood Invitational and the remarkable prowess of the preacher have to be viewed and appreciated.

At a tournament you could always spot the serious archers. They would show up a day or two early and shoot around the course a few times to learn its peculiar features. Each course was unique and had its own difficult uphill and downhill shots. Terrain, and the parabolic path of an arrow traveling only a couple of hundred feet per second, could combine to fool even the most skilled sight shooter who knew the exact distance to the target. And then there was the yardage itself. The course markings had to be accurate in order to have it certified. But the members of the host club maintained the range. In between certifications they were not always careful about whether shooting stakes got shifted a little one way or the other. Not much. Just enough to restore a bit of hometown advantage to a sport that most of them thought had become too precise and too exacting in the posting of distances and the use of calibrated sights.

It didn't matter so much at the shorter distances where the trajectory of the arrow was fairly flat. Even at the longer ranges, where the curving path of the arrow causes it to drop rapidly with distance, the effect was largely mental. That little loss of confidence suffered by a shooter who stops to question whether the yardage shown is really correct; whether the sight is set properly; whether he should compensate by holding a bit above or a bit below the center when the first arrow is a close miss. It is much easier to blame one's equipment, or the marking of the course, than it is to accept that the miss was a small lapse in technique, a breakdown in concentration, some inattention to the numerous little details of shooting. The shooter compensates. The next arrow misses too, and a collapse ensues. Once that mental door is opened, it can be hard to get it shut again. Through it more than one archer has walked out of a tournament—and out of the sport forever.

A few of the top archers made it a point not to show up early. As if to declare that they didn't seek—or need—any advantage. As if by that gesture of apparent disdain and nonchalance to cede outright any edge to their opponents. After all, at the national tournaments everyone had to shoot an unfamiliar course. If then, why not now? That's what it was all about, wasn't it—matching one's skill against the course and beating everyone else at it? This strategy was itself an attempt to gain a psychological edge, to undermine the confidence of those whose self-assurance was fragile enough to make them feel deep down that they needed, or at any rate wanted, some advantage, however slight. And sometimes it seemed to work.

But the preacher was not among any of the archers we have been discussing here. Some, only hearing of him later and not having gotten to see him perform, might be forgiven for wondering whether the preacher's peculiar abilities were even subject to the vicissitudes of this world.

The first day of the Invitational was a Saturday in one of those perfect years when Easter fell in mid-April, awash in a glorious renewal of life. The dogwoods were dazzling, the stunning profusion of pink and white blossoms made more spectacular by a mild winter and an early spring. The first group of archers set out on their circuit of the twenty-eight targets promptly at 8:00. At each ten-minute interval another group took their places on the shooting line at the first target, a maximum of four archers to a group, until all of the competitors were on the course. The final group would not finish until late afternoon. The more finicky shooters were slow and methodical. The out-and-out prima donnas always managed to hold up the flow, pausing to meticulously adjust equipment before each arrow, or to agonize over the scoring of every shaft—theirs or anyone else's—for which it could be questioned whether it was touching the next highest scoring ring. Or just to linger over some group of arrows well shot—especially if by doing so they might expect to nettle their opponents.

The preacher arrived late. Of course no one knew he was a preacher until he signed his entry form with that peculiar appellation. Even then the tournament secretary suspected something of a spoof, or a mild put-on, when he scrawled an almost illegible "Preacher Parsons" at the bottom of his completed card and handed it back to her. But with good humor, and in the spirit of accommodating yet one more of the little idiosyncrasies she had become accustomed to encountering from individuals who still shot bows and arrows in a world that long ago had put them aside and moved on to other pursuits, she looked over the form and said, "You'll have to hurry along, Preacher, if you expect to shoot. The final group is getting set right now over at the first target." Then she added, "Wait, you didn't put down what class you're shooting in." When she got nothing but a blank look from the preacher, she glanced at his bow and said, "I suppose you're shooting traditional," then marked his card and sent him on. "If you have questions, Preacher," she told him, "ask those two fellows you're shooting with. They'll help you."

The preacher took his place with the two men already at the shooting stakes. The course marshal checked their score cards and, at a signal from the woman that no one else was waiting to register, authorized them to begin.

There was something about the preacher, both in his manner and his appearance, that suggested someone often late, or at least often out of step. He was a youngish man of only medium build, but with powerful, rounded shoulders, thick wrists, and large rough hands. His face and neck and hands were deeply creased and weather-beaten and suggested someone much older, someone accustomed to years of hard labor out of doors. Nothing about his appearance would have suggested his indicated profession.

He wore heavy khakis spotted here and there by small tears, a stained blue denim shirt, and old work boots. His face was frozen in a sort of pleasant, bemused look that was as disarming as the complete absence of anything definite that it revealed. A shock of thick reddish-brown hair gave the impression, even when brushed aside, of going off in all directions. In spite of his inscrutable countenance and unruly mat of hair, there was an underlying earnestness about him, detectable in the pale gray eyes peering through lids narrowed in a sort of permanent squint. The general consternation conveyed by his appearance was accentuated by his habit, whenever at a loss for what to say, of saying nothing at all. He would remain silent behind that blank disarming stare, steely gray eyes boring into his questioner, and simply wait for whatever came next. Though once he got his bearings, the preacher could be charming in his own naive way.

"Where'd you get that bow, Preacher — at K-Mart?" One of the two men spoke when the preacher introduced himself. The preacher gave the man a long, inquisitive look.

"I don't rightly know where it come from," he said finally. "One of the deacons in the church give it to me. Complained that he was spending way too much time at it." The preacher paused as if thinking about something, then chuckled to himself. "His wife kept after him that it was the Devil's work. Finally got so that he had to get shed of it. My missus been after me to find a hobby, somethin' to keep me from bein' underfoot all the time. So I done us both a good turn and took it off his hands."

As suddenly as he had turned garrulous, the preacher retreated behind his inscrutable gaze and stood staring at his two companions.

"Nothing wrong with your bow, Preacher. Don't you mind him." It was the other man now who spoke. "Been doing much shooting, Preacher?"

"Just there at the pars'nage. I got me some straw bales out behind the church. Gits boring, though, shootin' by yourself."

"Well you ought'n be bored none here, Preacher," the first man said. "We all aim to see to that." The man smiled idiotically at the preacher. "Why don't we get this here show on the road?"

The other two men shot first. The preacher stood watching, absorbed in studying every detail, every little nuance, as though he were seeing something difficult and perplexing done correctly for the first time. The distance to the first target was forty-five yards. The terrain was flat and there was an unobstructed view all the way to the target butt. The two men were freestyle shooters. Each in turn adjusted his sight for the distance, placed an arrow underneath a thin, narrow strip of spring steel mounted on the side of the bow, came to full draw and anchored beneath the chin, aimed, and while holding the sight pin steady in the center of the target drew the point of the arrow slowly, almost imperceptibly, through the metal strip. The release occurred immediately at the metallic snap of the clicker against the side of the bow. Both men put all four arrows in the five-ring. Each had two in the black spot in the center and two in the adjacent white area outside of the spot but well inside the thin line that marked the outer limit of the highest scoring area.

Finally it was the preacher's turn. And the preacher, using a bow that most tournament archers would have considered, if not obsolete at least unsophisticated and out of fashion, with no sight and no clicker, and pulling the string not with the protection of a thin tab but with the ends of his thick meaty fingers encased in a stiff leather shooting glove, anchoring his drawing hand not beneath his chin in the manner of target archers but well up on the side of his face, and with the bow held not vertical but canted (but with aluminum arrows bequeathed to him by his predecessor that were as straight and as identical as modern technology could fashion them, and perfectly matched to his bow) drove all four of his arrows, one after another, into the black spot in the very center of the target.

"Sweet Jesus, George, what do we have here?" the first man exclaimed to his partner.

"My God," the other man gasped. "Preacher, how in hell did you do that?"

The preacher looked at the two men as if unsure whether to answer. "Why, I just took these here arrers and shot 'em into that there spot."

"Huh. I'll say you did, Preacher. Yessir, I'd say you did."

At that moment a faint murmur of excitement swept around the course. Perhaps it was the tournament official who happened to see the final threesome of the day shoot the first target. Perhaps it was the bystander making home movies who captured the preacher's first four arrows on film and gave us the only documented, though fragmentary, evidence that what people later remembered of that day could actually have occurred more or less the way they remembered it. Perhaps there was already some anticipation of it in the air before the preacher ever shot. However it came about, the awareness of those first four arrows, and the possibility that something quite strange and remarkable was taking place, made its way around the course almost before the preacher finished duplicating the exact same feat on the second and third targets.

That intriguing possibility formed just part of the larger drama being played out amid the dogwood blossoms. There were the usual mind games. Most of the archers had come with new equipment. Not because they couldn't shoot their old tackle just as well, but to sow the seeds of doubt that without the material trappings of progress no progress was possible. Best of all was a bow with some radical new feature — pre-stressed limbs for which greater speed could be claimed, or a new limb configuration for which improved stability was touted. Consistency and smoothness of draw — those were favorites too. The substance of any claim was less important than the claim itself, and the doubt that it planted in the minds of the other shooters.

Leading off that morning on the first target, Bill McConnell took his new metal-handle bow and put his first two arrows in the center spot. "Where'd those arrows go?" he asked, looking perplexed.

"Why, they're in the spot, Bill," someone assured him.

"I know that." He sounded impatient. "But where?"

"Low in the spot," the same voice answered. So Bill made quite a to-do of adjusting his sight and then proceeded to put the next two arrows right in the center of the spot. After that, one of his three companions shot his first arrow high in the three-ring and the next one at the very bottom of the target. By the time he recovered his composure several targets later he was out of contention.

Even as the preacher was setting out, one of the local club members, an affable, elderly archer named Willard Thomas, had just reached the midway point of the first fourteen targets, a downhill sixty-yard shot across a wide sloping depression that fell gently away from the shooting stakes and then rose abruptly right in front of the target. Willard had shot a bow for so many years that the last digit on the forefinger of his right hand had rotated forty-five degrees so that the flat side of the finger matched the angle made by the bowstring at full draw. Willard was an inveterate clicker-shooter. Early on he had developed aiming problems, unable to keep from releasing the string before he had the arrow aimed the way he wanted it. The clicker solved that problem by separating the release from aiming. Aiming was visual. Releasing was triggered by the sound (or by the feel) of the clicker slapping against the side of the bow, not by any visual cue. With the clicker Willard had no problem aiming. But don't let anyone snap a cigarette lighter near him when he had the bow partially drawn or someone was liable to get shot. Any sudden metallic click and he would shoot, ready or not.

That is, until he had consumed a couple of beers. Willard carried beer in the bottom of his ample quiver. By the second or third beer he no longer had an aiming problem and didn't need the clicker. That usually coincided with reaching this particular sixty-yard target. He would step up to the shooting stakes, announce ceremoniously to his shooting companions that this was *his* target, and proceed to score a perfect twenty points. From that point he became a formidable opponent and out shot a lot of younger, better archers who simply couldn't get their heads around what had just taken place.

A Florida archer named Gandy (or Handy, or Dandy, or something like that) had invented a new way of shooting using the point of the arrow as a sight bead, without having a sight on the bow, allowing him to compete against the traditional shooters but with all the advantages of a sight. For each distance he worked out a particular combination of where to place his fingers on the string and where to anchor his drawing hand on his face, that enabled him to always hold the point of the arrow directly on the spot he wanted to hit. He used two anchors, one below the chin for the longer distances and another at the corner of the mouth for the shorter yardage. To locate his fingers on the string he counted down the correct number of turns on the string serving. "String walking" they soon started calling it.

It was the same as having a sight on the bow, no doubt about it. From the moment they decided to post the distance to the target, it was inevitable that someone would think of it. It was perfectly legal too, though some questioned whether it was ethical. The rule book didn't say you couldn't aim. It only said you couldn't have a sight mounted on the bow. In this scheme the bow *was* the sight. The point of the arrow served as the front sight. The combination of anchor point and finger placement on the string adjusted the rear elevation of the arrow for the correct trajectory at each distance. Ingenious. Very. What upset everyone was that none of *them* had thought of it. Ethics be damned. They would all go home and learn the new technique themselves. Next year everyone would be using it.

A crowd had gathered to watch this phenomenon from Florida.

"Take a gandy at that, would you," one of them said.

"Yessir, seems like a right handy fella to me," remarked another.

"Oh, he's a real dandy all right," chimed in a third.

The object of all the attention was shooting in a group that included last year's winner, a North Carolina archer and current national champion named Necessary (or Not-so-scary, or Accessory, or something like that.) He was shooting as well as ever and falling steadily behind as his opponent pulled away toward a new course, if not a new national, record. Finally, in a fit of frustration following a close miss he slung his bow end over end out through the dogwood and redbud trees lining the sides of the trail. The bow bounced off several trees before coming to rest in a blizzard of pink and white petals drifting gently downward. "Now was that really *necessary?*" someone in the crowd quipped. The attention turned back to the other shooter, who at this point was competing only against himself and against what was possible. And against the freestyle shooters who were themselves in danger of being eclipsed by this new technique in the hands of an able practitioner.

And against the preacher, too. The rumor quickly spread that out there somewhere in the woods an unknown itinerant preacher, a country bumpkin, a hillbilly, a redneck hick, a nobody, had appeared from out of nowhere and proceeded to shoot a perfect score through the first fourteen targets; and was even then wrecking similar havoc on the next fourteen.

Still, it was only a rumor. On the eighty-yard walk-up target the preacher lost a full five points when his first arrow barely caught the bottom of the target bales. He had never even considered shooting at anything so far away. He lost another two points on the same target from seventy yards when his second arrow landed low in the three-ring, before finally figuring out the correct elevation and scoring five points each from sixty and fifty yards. And he dropped another two points on a difficult sixty-five-yard downhill shot, and two points on a treacherous fifty-five yarder across a deep ravine.

What was not a rumor was that he had a perfect score going on the final fourteen. It was also not a rumor that an ungodly number of his arrows landed in the black aiming spot in the center of the five-ring. And it was no rumor that when he finally signed his score card (which he let his shooting companions fill out for him because he had never done it before, though he totaled the final score himself and recorded it in bold numerals at the bottom before signing Preacher Parsons in his almost illegible scrawl) and turned it in, he posted the highest score of the day and sent tournament officials scrambling for their record books.

By the time the preacher was nearing the end of the course word of all these things had spread. An expectant crowd gathered at the final target, a short, thirty-five-yard, uphill shot. A steady buzz of excitement drowned out the bees feeding on the sourwood blossoms. The preacher shot last as he had throughout the day. The crowd was not disappointed. All four arrows were bunched in the center of the bulls-eye.

Then someone noticed what they thought was a peculiar pattern to the placement of the arrows, and afterwards retrieved the target face. A curious crowd gathered around. Sure enough. The neat, round punctures caused by the preacher's arrows took the form of a tiny cross in the center of the target.

Quickly a group scurried back along the shooting lanes to inspect the other targets. When they returned they brought with them several more that bore the same unmistakable pattern of a four-pointed cross in the middle. As they stood inspecting them someone asked the preacher if he would mind shooting again for the crowd. Clean targets were put up on the practice bales and the preacher shot several more ends, each at a fresh target. Each time there was the same peculiar pattern to the arrows.

"How in heaven's name do you do that, Preacher," someone asked.

The preacher looked at him quizzically. "Like I said. I just take these here arrers and shoot 'em into that there spot. I don't rightly know what else to tell you."

Just then the tournament secretary came hurrying over. "You'll have to be here early tomorrow, Preacher. We'll put you with the three highest scorers from today and start you all out first."

"Oh, I won't be here tomorrow," the preacher said. "Tomorrow's Easter Sunday. I got to hold services."

"But you can't quit now, Preacher. Not after what you did today."

The preacher remained impassive. "I'm afraid I'll have to," he said. "Besides, I've already learnt what I wanted to know."

"What's that, Preacher?" someone asked.

The preacher just stared from behind the inscrutable mask and walked away without answering.

Some of those targets hung in the clubhouse for years afterwards. Some people claimed that the arrow holes didn't really form a cross after all, or at least not in every case, and they produced other faces they said were from that day to prove their point. Others claimed that those were merely forgeries or fakes. There was even a rumor that when several of the authentic faces were inspected more closely, faint brown stains resembling dried blood could be seen along the edges of each of the four round holes forming the cross. Others scoffed at such a suggestion.

No one ever saw the preacher shoot again, not in public anyway, and not long afterwards he disappeared. Someone said that he took another church farther back in the hills, where they were too poor to shoot bows and arrows and would have thought that anyone who did was doing the Devil's work. Not long after that was when we first noticed the dogwoods beginning to die. Each spring fewer and fewer of the pink and white petals show up amid the redbud and sourwood blossoms. If something doesn't change, the dogwood trees will soon be gone. Nowhere will we have the delicate, brown-stained petals to serve as the Easter flower. Perhaps that just means that we won't need it anymore.

I watched him shoot that afternoon, a slight, modest, unassuming figure, in khakis and work boots and denim shirt, his simple plain-looking bow cradled loosely in one massive hand. I couldn't see anything obvious, or peculiar, about what he seemed to be doing, not in the way he stood or held his bow arm or aimed or released the string. Even his follow-through seemed unremarkable, almost indistinguishable. He just seemed to quit holding the string at some point. He didn't stand straight, but leaned slightly forward at the waist. His bow wasn't even canted the same on every shot. But the arrows kept finding their way, one after another, to the center of the target.

I remember talking to my father about it as we were driving home that evening. "Do you think the preacher will be the greatest archer ever some day?" I asked him.

"No," he said. "I don't think so."

"Why not?" I asked. "You saw him shoot."

"Yes, I know," my father replied. "But someday the preacher is going to learn how to miss. And when that happens, he will become just like the rest of us."

I suppose my father's comment is one of the reasons I still wonder sometimes if it really could have happened.

FIVE IN

"I'm telling you man, that's him." Ed motioned toward the shooter on lane seven. Only two other lanes were in use. The rest stood empty. Most of the regulars stayed away on a cold, dreary Sunday afternoon. Hunting season was over, and the indoor leagues shot on week nights. It was too soon yet for the few Las Vegas fanatics to start coming in on the weekends, trying to get ready for the big event of the indoor season.

Jim shook his head. "Naw, it couldn't be. Take a look at that guy. He's a bum. He looks like he's just coming off a three-day binge."

"I don't care. I've seen the pictures in the magazines, and that's him," Ed said.

The light in the shooting area was yellow and dim. There was good light on the targets, bright fluorescent and blue-white. Away from the targets the light was a dirty, dingy yellow that made it hard to get a good look at the features of the shooter on lane seven.

"Have you watched this guy shoot?" Jim said. "He's throwing arrows all over the goddamn place. That can't be him. This guy's a bum."

"It's him," Ed said. "Don't you see? The open stance, the high wrist, three fingers under? That's him all right."

"What would he be doing here? Tell me that, wise guy."

"It's a free country. He can go wherever he wants. Lots of people come to Albuquerque."

"You're crazy. Who's the bimbo?" Jim looked at the woman shooting on lane one.

"I don't know. I suppose she's with him."

"Take a look at that would you. What a case. She doesn't even know which end of the bow is up. It's not hard to imagine what he sees in her. She looks like a slut. And he looks like a bum."

"Not a bad looking slut," Ed said.

Everything about the woman on lane one seemed out of place. Her clothes were all wrong. They looked like they had been chosen for the single purpose of revealing and exaggerating what was already, without any help, quite a stunning figure. They weren't cheap clothes, but not stylish either, too tight and skimpy in all the wrong places where they didn't need to be. The way she was dressed would have been only slightly outrageous for someone trying to get picked up in a singles bar. Here it was merely incongruous and absurd. She was shooting inexpensive and ill-matched equipment from the pro shop. It was obvious she didn't have the slightest notion what she was doing. She had run her target out barely ten yards, at which she shot an occasional shaft that even less occasionally managed to hit the target butt, though not the target face itself. Those that missed skidded noisily along the concrete floor or ricocheted with a jarring metallic clang off the wall at the back of the lanes. She seemed absent and uninterested in the whole affair. Between arrows she sat and looked over at the shooter on lane seven.

"What a bimbo. Why does Harry let people like that in here?"

"Aw, she's just fooling around. It's good for business. Who knows, maybe she'll take up the sport," Ed said.

"Oh, I'll bet she's fooling around all right. Wonder what she sees in that bum?"

"I thought she was a bimbo."

"She is. But he's even more of a bum."

"I'm telling you, Jim, that's him."

"And I'm telling you, I'll bet I can kick his ass. Why don't you go and rent lane eight for us? We'll find out if he's a bum."

Ed walked back to the pro shop to reserve lane eight. He wrote the names Mackey and Wilson in the empty slot beside lane eight on the schedule board, then asked the man behind the counter, "Mike, who's that shooting on lane seven?"

"I don't know him," Mike said. "He came in asking for the boss. Said he's an old friend. When I told him Harry never comes in on Sunday anymore, he asked if he could shoot. Don't say anything about it to Harry, I didn't write him in on the chart. Said he didn't have any money on him. I've never seen him around before. I thought you might know."

"That's just it, I thought I recognized him. Never mind."

"Did you get a load of that cutie with him? Harry's going to be sorry he wasn't here to see that."

When Ed returned, Jim was shooting his first end. The shooter on lane seven stood watching him, waiting for Jim to finish before pushing the button that would start the target moving along the tracks to retrieve his arrows.

As soon as Jim released his fifth arrow, the stranger reached over and pushed the return button and stood watching the target roll toward him along the two parallel steel rails bolted to the concrete floor. When the cart halted abruptly at the end of the tracks he began pulling his arrows. They were all in the blue and white target face pinned to the center of the bale, but they were scattered. There was nothing that one could call a group, just five individual arrows that seemed to have each taken a different route from the bow to the target.

While Jim waited for his target to return Ed sat watching the stranger. All he had ever seen were a few small photographs in old magazines, but it sure as hell looked like him. Five times national bare-bow champion. The most difficult class, no sights or release aids of any kind allowed. The finest natural archer of all times, some said. At the peak of his form no one else had even been close. He regularly beat the freestyle shooters with their sights and all their gadgets. He hadn't invented string walking, but no one had ever equaled him at it. Ed had heard the stories. And some of them were backed up by scores in the record books. That much of it anyway was true. This guy did sort of look like a bum.

The stranger shot again. He seemed casual about it, almost unthinking, as if he were content just to release the arrows and watch them fly to the target with no concern about where they went. Ed studied him closely. All the elements of good form were there. He couldn't pick out anything in particular to criticize. None of the arrows was erratic and the five shafts he shot this time, like the five Ed had watched him pull from the target before, were scattered about the center. He was shooting borrowed equipment, but that wasn't it. The arrows were matched, and they flew well enough, but something was missing.

Ed watched him shoot another end, and then another, with the same results. He couldn't see any improvement, any change, he was just shooting the arrows and letting them go wherever they went. Ed watched Jim too. Now there was something interesting. Jim was shooting lousy scores, one raggedy-ass group after another. Three in the center spot and two just outside. Twice he saw him put four well inside the spot and then throw the last one way to the right, almost off the target face. What the devil is he up to? Ed wondered.

The stranger shot faster than Jim. Each time, while he stood waiting for Jim to finish before bringing the noisy platform clattering along the tracks to retrieve his arrows, the stranger watched Jim shoot. Ed noticed that he paid no attention to where the arrows were going. Instead he seemed intent on studying every move that Jim made, as though he were a coach about to instruct a pupil, or a student taking lessons himself. He was quick to avert his attention whenever he thought Jim might notice him watching.

After several ends, he waited until Jim had shot his final arrow and said, "You've got good form."

"You want to shoot together?" Jim asked.

"Sure, I guess so, why not? My name's David." The stranger offered Jim his hand.

"I'm Jim Mackey. My friend over there is Ed Wilson. You going to shoot with us, Ed?" Jim yelled above the noise of the target station lumbering along the rails.

"No, go ahead," Ed yelled back. "I might shoot after a while."

Jim walked over to the target on lane seven, took the blue and white face off the backstop, and mounted both faces on the target butt on lane eight.

"That about right for you?" Jim asked.

"Sure, I'm not particular."

Jim sent the cart lurching along the rails to the far end of the lanes. "Looks farther than twenty yards, doesn't it?" he said.

"It always looks farther indoors," the stranger replied, "or anytime you're trying to put them all in the center."

"Where you from? Jim asked. Haven't noticed you in here before."

"All over. Texas mostly. Just stopped by on my way through, hoping to catch Harry. Me and Harry go way back."

"Is that your wife?"

"Lola? Oh no." The stranger smiled. "We're just killing a little time together. Me and her don't go much farther back than the other night."

"She's sure a looker."

"Yeah, I guess so. She's a good sport anyway."

Ed sat and watched the two of them shoot. Jim was a 299 or a 298 shooter. He could put five arrows in the spot nine times out of ten. He never dropped more than one or two points a game. Pretty good for a finger shooter. About once a season he managed to put

67

together a perfect 300 round, five arrows in the three-inch circle twelve consecutive times. Tonight he was playing another kind of game. Ed hadn't seen him get five in yet. He alternated between shooting ragged groups and tight groups with one or two outliers, never more than four in the blue dot in the middle of the blue and white face.

The stranger kept watching Jim shoot. He became more deliberate now in his own shooting. Ed watched, fascinated, as the arrows began to converge on the center of the target face. Soon he was getting three in, though they were spread all over the blue three-inch circle and the other two were always well out. He didn't improve beyond that.

The stranger walked back to the pro shop. Ed could see him talking to Mike behind the counter and they seemed to be doing something to the bow. Mike disappeared into Harry's office and when the stranger returned he had another bow, the demo model that Harry kept hanging on his wall for prospective customers to try.

He walked back to the shooting lane, said something to Jim, and shot his next end. The results were about the same as before.

Suddenly Ed saw it. He had been paying too much attention to the ones that went in. The two arrows outside the five-ring were touching. He should have noticed it earlier when the stranger reached up with one hand and pulled them both out of the target at the same time as if they were a single arrow.

That son-of-a-gun, Ed thought. He watched him closely this time. The first arrow went high and to the right. The next two were in the spot but not close to each other. The fourth arrow slammed into the first one on its way into the target face. The fifth arrow hit by itself low in the center.

"Why, you-son-of-a-gun," Ed muttered.

After that end the stranger sat down and watched Jim shoot. "You want to shoot for score?" Jim asked him.

"If you want to, sure," the other man said.

"I'll get us some clean target faces," Jim said. He walked to the pro shop and came back with two new targets, pinned them side by side to the backstop, and sent the cart clanking twenty yards down the rusty steel tracks.

"I don't know about you," Jim said, "but keeping score always helps me concentrate." Jim handed the man a blank score card. "We don't have to shoot a complete game. We'll just take it one end at a time."

"Whatever you want to do," the stranger replied.

Jim shot first. They alternated shooting, each one watching the other shoot between arrows. Jim matched whatever score the stranger shot. After the first two ends of twenty-three apiece, Jim shot a twenty-three on his third end. The stranger surprised him by putting his fifth arrow in the spot to go up by one point. They each shot twenty-four on the next end.

"Hell," Jim said, "it seems like I can't do anything unless there's something riding on it. Why don't we make this more interesting? How about a dollar a point?"

"Whoa—too rich for me," the stranger said. "I'm wondering how I'm going to get home as it is. I can't afford to take that kind of chance."

"Fifty cents then." Ed paused. "You could win a stake."

"Oh no. I been watching you shoot. I couldn't win a stake if we was to go twenty dollars a point."

"C'mon," Jim said. "I was hoping to get the juices flowing."

"Count me out. I'm already over my limit. I'm sponging off Lola as it is."

Jim looked over at Lola who had stopped shooting and had been wandering about aimlessly, in and out of the pro shop, talking at times to Mike, and who now sat reading a Playgirl magazine in the dimly lighted area behind the shooting lanes. She looked bored.

"What if it didn't cost you anything?" Jim said.

"What do you mean?"

"I mean, what about her?"

"What about her?" the stranger asked.

"What if you put her up for your part?"

"You don't know Lola, fella. She may look like that, but she's not going to be part of any penny-ante bet. She'd be one pissed-off broad."

"No, I mean let's make it real interesting. I'll put up fifty bucks against Lola. On the next five arrows—winner take all. If you win you get your stake. If I win I get a turn with Lola."

"I couldn't dump her like that."

"No need to. She won't have to go any farther than the back of my van out in the parking lot. What do you say?"

"I don't know, I could sure use fifty bucks. What if I get lucky and shoot 'em all in, but you're better'n you been letting on, and you do too. Then I'd have to get lucky enough to do it all over again. Don't seem much like my kind of odds."

"We'll use the new faces—with the divided center spot. In case of a tie the one with the most arrows in the inner ring wins. How about it?"

"I'd have to talk to Lola."

"Take your time," Jim said.

The stranger walked back to where Lola was reading her magazine. Jim wandered over to Ed.

"What's going on?" Ed asked.

"I'm about to get me some of that." Jim nodded toward Lola.

"Oh yeah, what's it going to cost you?"

"The way I figure it, nothing."

"And if you're wrong?"

"There's fifty bucks riding on it."

"Fifty bucks! On what?"

"On the next five arrows, most hits in the new scoring ring wins."

"I think there's something you should know, Jim," Ed said. "That's him. I'm sure of it."

"I don't give a damn if he's Robin Hood—I can beat him. I've been stringing him along. You saw him. He's shooting the best he can."

"All right, good buddy, don't say I didn't warn you. You're on your own."

Jim went to get the new target faces. Ed looked over to where the stranger stood talking to Lola. She appeared animated and agitated, began waving her arms, and started to leave. The man took hold of her and was trying to calm her down. She pulled away and made it to the front door before he caught up with her. The two of them disappeared outside. After a couple of minutes they came back in. Lola sat down in a chair by the door, turned her head to one side away from the lanes, and sat staring at the wall.

The stranger came back to lane eight, picked up the borrowed bow, and walked toward the pro shop. Jim met him midway.

"Where you going?"

"I talked her into it, but I'm not going to ask her to put it on the line for a lousy fifty bucks. The bet's off."

"Wait a minute. You agreed. If she's willing, why not? What do you have to lose?"

"I'm not going to do it."

"All right, I'll double it. A hundred bucks. But that's it. She doesn't look worth any more than that to me."

70

The stranger appeared to be thinking.

"She going to pay up if you lose?" Jim asked.

"She'll do it. Lola's a good sport. But she won't like it."

"That's okay. I'll enjoy it more that way."

The two men walked back to the shooting line. Jim put the two new target faces on the backstop and pushed the button to send the cart toward the concrete wall at the far end of the building. The two men flipped a coin to see who would shoot first.

Jim won the toss. He put five arrows, one after another, in the blue center spot. Three of them looked tight enough to be inside the inner scoring ring. From twenty yards neither man could see the thin white line that divided the blue center into two concentric circles.

Jim looked at the other man. "You want to see me do it again?" There was no hint of a taunt in his voice. Just an air of confidence and triumph.

"I want to see your money," the stranger said.

"What?"

"Let's see the hundred bucks before I shoot. I owe Lola that much."

Jim smiled but didn't say anything. He took out his wallet and laid five twenty-dollar bills on the scoring table.

"Is that okay?"

"That's fine."

The stranger turned to the target and methodically fitted an arrow to the string, then drew, aimed, and released. The arrow hit the exact center of the blue circle. In a smooth steady rhythm, fixed and machine-like, he nocked, drew, aimed, and released four more arrows. Each of them went to the same spot. The five arrows formed a single dense mass covering the very center of the blue bulls-eye swimming against a white background. Even from where he sat Ed knew there was no question. All of them were well inside the smaller inner circle of the blue center.

"Damn right," Ed muttered. "I knew it."

The stranger looked at Jim. "Want to see *me* do it again?"

He reached down and moved the twenty-dollar bills, one at a time, over to the edge of the table, as if matching them one by one with the five arrows he had just shot, before picking them up, folding them, and slipping them into his shirt pocket.

"I'll give you a chance to win it back. But you'll have to talk to Lola. This money's hers."

He picked up the borrowed bow and started to leave. "You're

71

a damn good shot, mister, but if you're going to hustle somebody you have to learn to pay attention." He turned and walked off. Jim watched him go without saying a word.

Lola came over to meet him. She was smiling. When she reached the stranger she threw her arms around his neck. He took the neatly folded twenty-dollar bills out of his pocket and counted them out one at a time into her hand.

Ed walked over to where they stood.

"Say, did you use to be David Bower?" Ed asked.

The man looked at him.

"No...that was someone else...," he started to answer.

"Why sure he did, Sugar," Lola broke in. "He still is, can't you tell? Why, oh my, yes—he sure is."

"C'mon, Lola, let's go get something to eat," the man said.

AT THE TOP OF THE WORLD

A blue bottle fly, its metallic color shining iridescent in the bright sunlight, buzzed against the plate glass at the front of the donut shop. Sunshine streaming in through the broad expanse of glass had heated the stagnant air until the inside of the shop felt warm and drowsy. At one end of the serpentine counter that snaked its way along the length of the room an old man sat slumped on a stool. His massive, close-cropped head rested face down on the backs of rough, puffy hands spread flat on the Formica counter top. A stubborn growth of graying stubble covered his sunken cheeks. Near his bowed head sat a saucer with a cup of tepid coffee and a half-eaten donut.

Louise, the waitress, busied herself behind the counter. Outside, a cold blustery west wind swept out of a towering blue sky. Across the street, rows of gaily colored pennants strung above a used car lot flapped and whipped in the brisk wind. The broad street was almost deserted. Both sides were lined by budding sycamore trees and beds of blooming jonquils. A block away a small group of parked cars clustered about the front of a trim white church. Lilacs and yellow forsythia bushes bloomed in the churchyard. The constant snap and crackle of the flapping banners almost drowned out the sounds of singing and the wavering tones of a piano playing hymns.

Louise methodically went through the motions of wiping down the length of the counter for the third time. The old man had been the only customer since she opened. She prepared to pour out the old coffee and make new.

"Want me to warm up your coffee, Walter?" She asked it mechanically, without looking up. The man didn't reply. His eyes were closed. He breathed slowly, but evenly, and appeared to be asleep.

73

Louise dumped the carafe of coffee into the stainless-steel sink, poured ground coffee into a paper filter, plopped it in the basket of the automatic coffee maker, and flipped the switch. Within seconds the sound of gurgling water was followed by a stream of darkening liquid pouring into the glass pot underneath.

While she was occupied, a tall black man in a suit and tie and wearing a felt fedora and dark overcoat entered the shop. In long even strides he walked briskly to the rest rooms at the far end of the shop. When he returned he took a seat at the opposite end of the counter from Walter. He took off his hat and placed it beside him on the counter top.

"Morning, Louise."

"Good morning, John."

"How long has he been like that?" The man nodded toward Walter but kept his eyes fixed on Louise. Louise avoided looking at him.

"Ever since he came in about an hour ago," she said, lowering her voice as she glanced toward Walter.

"He ate a few bites, then fell asleep. Didn't say hardly a word. I couldn't get him to talk about a thing."

The man lowered his voice too. "I thought we had an agreement, Louise." He sounded peevish. "I asked you not to give him any more donuts. The poor man's got to eat right." He looked over at the hunched form slumped against the counter.

He kept his voice low. "When he comes in, fix him a can of soup or some beef stew or something. I told you, I'll pay for it. Just keep track of what he owes." His tone was accusing. "Mike won't object, will he?" Mike was the owner of the shop.

"He didn't want anything else," Louise replied. "I can't make him eat it. Better he eats part of a donut than nothing at all."

She turned away and began taking cups and bowls from the dishwasher and stacking them on the shelf behind her.

The man sighed. "I'll have the usual whenever you get time, Louise," his voice now conciliatory.

Louise did not respond but continued taking dishes from the machine and putting them on the shelf. Though on the verge of being plump, the waitress was young and still pretty. Her full figure suggested a certain voluptuousness, accentuated by a round mouth and full, pouty lips heavily rouged. The dark blue eye shadow and long black hair piled on the back of her head were in sharp contrast to her pale skin. The white polyester uniform she wore fit too snugly and the outlines of her undergarments were discernible against the sheer material of the skimpy, tight- fitting dress.

As a man and a woman came through the swinging glass doors, Louise picked up three cups and set them upright on the counter. She poured one cup full of coffee and took it, along with a donut from the display case in front of the entrance, to John who sat now bent over a folded newspaper.

"Thank you, Louise," John said without looking up. He said it flatly and nonchalantly with no hint of resentment.

The other two cups Louise took and sat in front of the man and the woman.

"Coffee?" she asked, then filled both cups without waiting for a reply. The man and the woman had been talking in low tones since they entered. Now the woman laughed quietly and the man looked up at Louise. He watched her as she returned the coffee pot to its hot plate and then brought napkins and silverware.

The woman asked for milk for the coffee. The man continued to watch Louise. Her nipples stood out against the tight dress and the man stared at them as she returned with their donuts. The woman kicked him under the counter. He diverted his eyes, then turned toward the woman and smiled. She laughed quietly.

The man kept glancing at Louise whenever he thought no one was watching, and twice more the woman caught him at it. Finally she nudged him and said, "Bob, please," under her breath but loud enough to be heard, and he grinned and leaned over and kissed her on the mouth. She put her hand in his lap beneath the counter. He whispered something in her ear and they both laughed and she kept her hand resting out of sight in his lap.

All at once the old man woke, heaving, and spit something up on the counter. Grabbing a handful of cloths, Louise hurried over to clean up the mess. Walter, fully awake now, began coughing violently, threatening to fall off the stool. Louise handed him a clean towel. The man and the woman looked away as the black man in the suit and tie walked past to steady the old man from behind.

"Walter, how are you doing? How long has it been since you had something to eat?" He asked it loudly, leaning over to speak directly into Walter's ear.

"I ate something this morning," Walter said when he had stopped coughing. He picked up a napkin, coughed once more, and spit a wad of mucous into the crumpled paper. Louise took it from him.

"I don't mean those damn donuts, Walter. They're no good for you. I mean real food. Why don't you let Louise fix you a bowl of soup, for goodness sake? You know you've got to eat, Walter. You won't ever get your strength back unless you eat right."

Walter lowered his head back down to the counter without answering. Louise brought him a fresh cup of coffee and sat it beside him. She stood looking at him.

"Can I get you something else, Walter? Would you like some hot soup? How about a sandwich? I can make you a ham sandwich if you want." She took the towel from where he had laid it on the counter. Walter didn't answer. He sat with his head forward on the counter as if he were asleep. John stood and watched him for a while, then shook his head at Louise and returned to his seat. He kept an eye on Walter for a few moments then resumed reading his paper.

The woman at the counter leaned her head against the man's shoulder and rubbed the small of his back with her hand. He slid his hand down and squeezed her thigh. Louise brought the coffee pot over. "More coffee?" she asked. The man pushed both cups toward her, and his eyes again traced the rounded outlines visible through the thin dress. Louise did not return his glances. Her eyes met the woman's as she turned to go.

Walter sighed heavily in his sleep, if he was asleep, but otherwise he did not move. For a while the only sound was the steady, rasping, aggravating buzz of the bottle fly bumping into the thick plate glass. John and Louise talked in low tones at the other end of the counter and he took money out of his wallet and gave it to her.

"When he wakes up see if he will eat something," the man at the counter overheard him tell Louise. "Give him another donut, I suppose, if he won't eat anything else. But try to get him to eat some soup." He picked up his hat and paper and left.

A customer, dressed for church, came in and sat a short distance from the man and the woman. He nodded toward them as he glanced around the shop. The woman took her hand out of the man's lap. The customer seemed not to notice. The man continued stealing glances at Louise as she went about her work. Walter sighed audibly and then raised up and looked around at nothing in particular. He took the coffee cup in both hands and, shaking, got it to his mouth and drank several gulps. Louise brought the pot over and poured him more. Unsteadily, he turned and stood, bracing himself against the counter. The exertion left him breathing hard. He steadied himself by holding on to the counter with one hand.

"Where you going, Walter?" the waitress asked him. Walter started for the door without answering. Louise looked around at the man beside the woman, and the man got up and came over to Walter, taking him by the arm.

"Can I help you, sir?" he asked.

"I'm going outside to wait," Walter said. The man supported him by the arm and looked around at the woman, then at Louise.

"Don't you have a coat? That wind out there's pretty cold."

"I don't need one," Walter said. "He'll be here soon."

He continued to shuffle toward the door. The younger man held the swinging door open while the old man went through it and into the dead air space between the inner and outer doorways. He let the first door go and opened the outer door and held it open against the wind while Walter slowly made his way outside. A car was parked beside the street a short distance from the entrance and Walter motioned him toward it. The man had not noticed the car when he came in. Someone had driven it up on the curb and left it beside the walk where there was no actual parking place. He opened the car door with one hand while steadying Walter with the other. On the front seat lay a heavy woolen coat.

"Here, put this on," he said.

Walter held out first one arm and then the other as he leaned against the car door to steady himself, then eased himself onto the edge of the front seat out of the wind while the younger man buttoned the coat for him. The old man's breath had a medicinal odor that he thought he had smelled before, but he couldn't remember exactly if, or when or where, so he wasn't sure. When the man finished buttoning the coat, Walter sat motionless on the edge of the seat with his feet resting flat on the ground outside the car. The physical exertion had left him exhausted. The open door shielded him from the wind, and he sat in the sun. Still, he'll get cold sitting there like that, the man thought. Walter sat staring at the ground without speaking. The man did not know what to say or do. He did not want to go and leave the old man there by himself.

"Are you all right?" he asked after a while.

The question seemed awkward and inappropriate as soon as he asked it. Walter didn't respond. He sat motionless, his head down. He could have been asleep, and the man wondered if perhaps he had dozed off again.

He tried again, louder this time. "Wouldn't you be more comfortable inside?" he asked. Then after a pause, "Who are you waiting for?"

"Paul will be along soon," Walter said. "He left the car here for me. I can wait right here until he gets back."

He sat, leaned forward, on the end of the seat with his feet still on the ground, as if about to get out of the car, except that he stayed crouched down behind the open door out of the wind and kept one big hand on the arm rest to support himself. Across the street the strings of colored pennants waving above the used car lot crackled and snapped in the breeze like flags flying at a fair or carnival. The fluttering noise they made broke up the smooth sound of the wind in the man's ears. He thought they looked cheerful in the bright sunshine against the clear blue of the desert sky. He could smell the lilacs blooming in the churchyard.

The sun shone through the car window onto Walter's bowed head. The man held his open hand in the sunshine just above the old man's head, out of the wind. It did not feel warm to him, but the old man's head with its close-cropped hair and wrinkled skin and his eyelids drooping shut reminded him of a lizard sunning itself on a rock. He glanced at the mountains in the distance swimming in the sunlight and thought of the gray granite boulders strewn about the foothills, and of the blue-tail lizards scurrying over them to dive out of sight in the cool sand underneath, and of the sage and chamisa and asters that would soon be blooming there. Even with his coat on he was cold standing in the wind, and thinking about lizards scampering in the hot sun did not make him feel any warmer. He wanted to go back inside. But it did not seem the right thing to do to leave the old man sitting out there alone in the cold with no one to keep an eye on him.

He glanced toward the donut shop. The woman was leaned over the counter talking to Louise. No one inside was looking to see what had happened to Walter, or him. He shifted his weight from one leg to the other. The gravel beside the car crunched beneath his feet. Just then the old man sat up straight in a sudden paroxysm of coughing that finally ended when he spit a wad of yellow mucous on the ground and slouched back into his slumped-over position on the edge of the seat behind the open car door.

"How long have you been sick?" he asked. It wasn't the question he wanted to ask. What he really wanted to know was what was wrong with the old man. But he couldn't think of any way of asking it that wouldn't be awkward or embarrassing. So he asked this other question instead.

"Have you been sick long?" When Walter did not respond, he tried again. "Can I get you anything? More coffee? Why not go back inside where you'll be warmer? We could wait in there. You could get warm and have something to eat."

Walter mumbled something in reply.

"What's that?" He drew closer to hear.

"They ruined me," he thought he heard the old man mumble.

"What? Who did?"

"They ruined me. I'm just no good anymore."

He had to lean close to hear what the old man was half whispering, the words swept away by the wind almost as fast as the sounds came out of his mouth. Another fit of coughing interrupted and left Walter gasping to get his breath. The man kept silent and waited.

"I got the cancer." He spoke in a hoarse raspy whisper. "They cut me open, but it didn't work. I still got it." He paused. "I haven't been good for anything since."

"Castrated me. Never even asked. Just did it while I was out. Ruined me too. Left me no good for anything anymore." He spoke slowly, as if carefully measuring the effort needed for each word. "I never told them they could do that, they just did it. I didn't even know they were going to. Said they told me, but they sure didn't. I'd have never let them ruin me that way. Don't never let them do it to you."

He sat looking straight ahead. The man had no trouble hearing him now.

"Medicine keeps me from holding on to my food." He paused again to catch his breath. Then he sighed. "I used to love coming here Sunday mornings, for a donut and a cup of coffee. Nothing's good any more. I'm just ruined."

The man stood listening and thinking. He squatted down beside the open door to be on a level with the old man who sat half turned, not looking at him or at anything in particular, staring vacantly ahead at the hard-packed earth and gravel beside the car. He squatted there in silence for a long time, peering at the form huddled on the seat in front of him. When the old man started speaking again, he at first had trouble picking the words out of the sound of pennants snapping and crackling in the wind.

"They don't know," he mumbled. "The ones that did it, them that cut me, they don't know how it feels. Nobody can know what it

79

is to be ruined like that. Paul understands. He's got it too. He knows what it's like." He was talking to no one now. Then after a while he added, "He'll be along directly."

The old man closed his eyes and soon he was breathing evenly again. He could have been asleep but he held firmly to the car door with one massive puffy hand, the other resting limply on his knee, and the man knew that he was not asleep.

The man didn't know what he could do, or say. Even if he had thought of something he would not have said it now since it seemed wrong to intrude where he knew he had no business, where silence seemed the only allowable response.

He stood up again, taking care not to shift his feet in the gravel or to make any sound that might disturb the old man. He thought the gaily colored flags flapping in the breeze seemed brighter and louder now than before. He looked up. The sky was the sort of intense blue that one found only in high deserts. In every direction he looked he could see a hundred miles. In the distance, thermal gradients in the moving air distorted the images and colored the horizon a thin strand of pale silver suspended wavering between earth and sky.

The bottomless blue of the sky overhead was reassuring, and the sun felt warm on his face despite the wind. Even the cold wind whipping through his hair felt good, he thought. The breeze brought occasional whiffs of a fragrance that reminded him of hyacinths, along with another scent, less distinct, that he did not immediately recognize.

One slow, deliberate step at a time he backed away from the car toward the sidewalk and the entrance to the donut shop. I'll get him another cup of coffee, he told himself, and another donut. By then maybe he'll want to eat something.

Back inside he took his seat on the stool beside the woman. She reached out and put her hand against his cheek.

"You're cold."

"Not really. I'm fine."

He ordered them each another donut and a fresh cup of coffee. Then he asked Louise to fix a cup for Walter. The woman put her hand back in his lap below the counter and rubbed the inside of his leg. When he looked over at her she fixed her eyes on his and pushed her cupped hand up against him. He looked away to where Louise, her back turned, was pouring coffee into three clean cups. The woman squeezed softly, still staring at his face. Just then, through the front of the shop, he saw a tall slender young man in a heavy mackinaw standing beside the car. Walter had turned and was sitting now straight ahead with his legs and feet inside the car. The young man in the mackinaw closed the car door. He stood for a moment looking in at Walter through the car window. Then he went around to the driver's side, got in, and drove away.

AT THE BEACH

I sat watching a barefoot man and woman on the beach. They were digging for clams at low tide, out where the retreating surf left long fingers of foamy froth seeping into the wet sand glistening in the morning sun. The man was young and trim and muscular, his thick arms uncovered and tan from long exposure to wind and sun. His straight sandy hair was stiff and cropped close and covered his head densely. The woman was large and heavy and frowzy. She wore ill-fitting pantaloons and a baggy blouse that draped loosely over her shoulders and waist. Her tangled unkempt hair waved and tossed in the sea breezes. But there was a certain cat-like quickness and raw sensuality about her movements that belied her bulky, frumpish appearance. She moved swiftly, easily, with a lithe, supple grace and agility. She beat the smooth wet sand about her with a short-handled shovel until she located the tell-tale dimple in the surface that betrayed the location of a retreating razor clam, then hurriedly shoved the blade of her shovel beneath it and quickly pried it up before it could sink deeper in the sand, and thrust it into a limp cloth sack that hung at her side. Her movements were lively and vigorous, and were practiced and sure and skillful.

In her excursions she veered sharply away from the man, wandering first left then right, but constantly hovered about his position. Each time she secured a clam she strode forcefully over to show him and they stood for a few moments in lively animated conversation. Then she dropped the clam in the pail of water the man carried and veered away again as abruptly as she had come. The man's movements were slower and more deliberate and adhered to a straighter path along the water's edge. As I watched they gradually diminished to mere specks far down the beach, still beating the wet sand and digging for clams.

I sat alone, quietly watching them through binoculars out the window of the trailer. They were quartering away and their backs were toward me. Suddenly the woman turned and walked briskly up behind the man and dropped her sack and shovel at his feet. She stood pressing against him, one hand resting on his shoulder, her head thrust forward over the other shoulder, peering down at the front of him. The man held his hands in front of him, extended below his waist. He stood with head bowed and stared down toward his feet.

She stood looming over him, almost obscuring him from view, motionless, watching him intently. Her entire posture was one of rapt fascination and complete curiosity. They remained like that for a long time. Finally, I saw him move his hands again and he turned towards her. For a brief moment she wrapped her arms around him in a tight embrace. Then they separated and spoke and seemed to be laughing and enjoying the moment.

I remember thinking to myself how lucky they were, how lucky to have each other and to be there together enjoying that beautiful day on the beach. And then thinking how lucky I was to be there too; how fortunate I was to see them. Many other things happened on that beach that are gone now from memory. But that scene of her watching him enthralled and of their laughing, animated conversation afterwards remains indelibly clear in my mind.

As I think back upon it, I realize it is one of the memorable instances of my life, one that I have never mentioned to anyone, but one I have recalled many times since.

AN AWAKENING

He woke sometime during the night. It was dark and he could make out only a few vague forms close by in the bedroom. He could see nothing in the hall beyond. There was no moon and he couldn't discern anything at all in the blank darkness outside the bedroom window. He knew it was not time to set out yet and that he needed to get as much sleep as he could. So he willed himself to wake up nearer daybreak, the way he knew he would if he willed it, and went back to sleep. When he woke later it was still dark outside, only now the darkness was not the same everywhere but took on various muted shapes. He could make out the first faint graying outlines of nearby trees and the indistinct forms of houses beyond.

He sometimes imagined that the world was being created anew each morning as it emerged from darkness and some things were always changed from the way they had been the day before, but that one had to look closely and even then it was sometimes not possible to see what was different. He even imagined that it might be possible to will the changes that one wanted, the way he could will himself to wake up at the right time in the morning. He liked to sit and watch the day break and think about what might have changed. This morning he knew he would not have time for that. Instead he thought about what he planned to do. But he knew he did not have time even for that, and that if he thought about it any further he might not go through with it.

He slipped out of bed and crept quietly down the hall to the bathroom. If anyone heard him now they would only assume he had gotten up to go to the bathroom and would not suspect anything. Once back in the bedroom he closed the door, being careful not to click the latch, and quickly got dressed in the clothes he had laid out before going to bed. From the closet floor he took a canvas knapsack

84

in which the day before he had put an apple, an orange and a banana, along with a peanut butter and jelly sandwich wrapped in wax paper. On the closet shelf he found a full box of three-inch .410 gauge shotgun shells, removed three of the shells from the box and put them in the outer pocket on the back of the knapsack, then placed the box with the remainder of the shells back on the shelf. Taking the whole box, or even more than the three shells, meant going beyond a self-imposed limit that made him uncomfortable. A few shells were one thing. The whole box seemed a much more serious transgression, even a violation of trust. He also slipped an empty spent shell that he had saved from the last time he went shooting with his father into his pants pocket. He would need it later for signaling.

He wore faded jeans and a stained short-sleeve shirt and well-scuffed, unpolished shoes, what his mother referred to as his play clothes and he called his old clothes, as distinct from his school clothes and his Sunday best, and which he always wore whenever there was any expectation of work or play that could result in getting dirty. Every afternoon when he came home from school he was required to change into his play clothes in order that his mother might maintain on her limited budget the standard of dress she deemed essential for school wear. He was most comfortable and at ease in his old clothes. He identified them with the time he spent wearing them. He didn't take a jacket or give any thought to a hat. It was late spring, almost summer, and unlikely to rain, and he knew the day would be hot although it would be pleasant enough until the sun was well up. He had not thought beyond that time frame.

Outside he could begin to see gray shapes more distinctly in the darkness and he knew it was time to go. He unlatched the screen on the open window and carefully lowered the knapsack to the ground beside the driveway. Finally, he took a single-shot .410 gauge shotgun from where it stood in the rear corner of the closet, and working the latching lever behind the hammer broke open the action to verify, as his father had taught him always to do, that the chamber was empty, just as he had already done several times before bringing the gun into the house and taking it to his room and standing it in the closet, then closed the action and locked the barrel back in place. He stood the locked gun on the ground beside the knapsack and leaned it against the side of the house. Then being very careful to make no noise he climbed through the window to the ground below, holding on to the screen to prevent it from slamming shut.

He put on the knapsack and draped the shotgun over his

shoulder with the barrel held forward in his right hand the way he had been taught to carry it. He did not envision loading the gun. There would be no need for that. That too would be a breach of trust. He walked the few short steps to the rear of the house and across the back yard to the opposite side. He did not dare take a chance on passing the open bedroom window beside which his father slept, even in the dark. One night his father, always a light sleeper, had seen the dim outline of a figure pass by his window three times. After the third time, he got out of bed and taking his pistol from the bureau drawer groped his way in the dark to the living room where he sat with his arms draped across the back of a chair, pistol in hand, aimed at the front door, waiting to see if the prowler would try to enter the house. The front door was never locked. But the doorknob didn't work properly and was stiff and difficult to turn. The prowler tried the knob several times then apparently concluded the door must be locked and gave up. If he had only pushed against it, the door would have swung open and his father might have shot him. As it was, his father sat and watched out the window as the man slowly walked away through the yellow glow of the streetlight two houses down the street. No one ever pursued the matter any further. He wasn't sure his father had even told anyone. He wondered sometimes what might have happened if the man had entered the house, and he always concluded that it was not an easy thing to decide.

He stood concealed in the deep shadow of the pecan and oak trees in the wide side yard and got his bearings. The sky was becoming noticeably lighter in the east. Daylight was approaching faster now, even since he had climbed through the window. He knew he had to go while he could still use the remaining darkness to conceal his movements. He walked the length of the side yard to the front of the house and stopped, leaning against the trunk of a massive pin oak beside the street. He stood there looking all around for any sign of movement before crossing the street and entering the shadows between the two houses immediately opposite. No one would see him there. He slipped past the houses and through the back yards into the gravel alleyway that ran behind the houses on that side of the street. He would go the rest of the way along the alley, which was farther from the houses bordering it than was the street in front.

He walked along the alley in the half-light, stopping often to look and listen. The sound of his footsteps in the gravel made him cautious. A wall of hedges and shrubbery screened the alleyway in most places from the back of the houses along both sides. He knew he would probably not be seen through the foliage even in daylight. There were lilacs and redbuds and hedges of box elder and intermittent patches of cane. Beyond them flowers were beginning to bloom in the back yards and gardens. He was aware of not knowing the names of most of them. He had never had a knack for keeping straight the names of plants, flowers in particular. He knew many of the deciduous trees, especially the native ones he found in the woods, because they were in the field guides his mother had given him. But he was not good with plants, unlike birds, all of which he could identify, many from their songs and calls alone. This morning he had already heard a house finch, a song sparrow, a robin, a mockingbird and a cardinal. When he reached the bayou he knew there would be meadowlarks and red-winged blackbirds and blue jays and bobwhite quail. He prided himself on his identification and knowledge of birds. He had started a species list keeping track of all the birds he had identified, noting where and when he had recorded each one. He knew the habits of most, the kinds of nests they built and the color and size of the eggs they laid.

Before long he came to a white two-story house unshielded by foliage from the alley. He could now see clearly even though it was not fully light. He knelt in the alley at the edge of the yard and took the spent shotgun shell from his pocket. Placing the edge of the open end against his lower lip he blew three short shrill blasts. It was the signal they had agreed upon. He watched the rear of the house for any sign of someone coming out. When he decided no one was going to emerge, he blew three more blasts, longer and louder this time, then waited again. Still no one appeared. He did not know what might have gone wrong. In the quiet dawn the high-pitched whistles could be heard a long way. He was afraid to make them any louder, or to signal yet again. Someone else might hear them and see him crouching there with a gun and wonder what he was doing. Perhaps he forgot to leave the window open. Perhaps his parents had found out. Or perhaps it had all been just idle talk. Maybe he had never intended to carry through with the plan and join him when he signaled. It was, after all, his plan. He had thought of it and suggested it; and now he would have to carry it out by himself.

Or he could turn back before it was too late. He would have a perfect excuse. The plan had been for the two of them to go together. He could hide the shotgun in the bushes and come back for it later when he could get it back in the house unnoticed. In the meantime no one would know it was gone. It stood in the back of the closet where no one ever looked. The only time he was allowed to have it out was when his father took him shooting on weekends, and since they had just been, that wouldn't happen again for a while. He could leave the knapsack with the gun. It was almost fully light, though still well before sunrise, and his father would be up by now. But he might still get back before he was missed. If they were already looking for him he could simply say he had gotten up early to go out and look at birds. His mother would scold him for not asking permission but it was at least reasonable. They had come to expect the unusual from him. He could work out later how to sneak the gun and knapsack back into his room. The web of deception he would have to weave to explain his actions spun out of control in his mind. No, he thought, I can't do it. It would mean lying. Worst of all he would be lying to himself and that he knew he would not do. He would rather be punished for something he had honestly done than be punished for a lie or have to live with the knowledge of it.

It was fully light now. The sun would rise soon. He had kept his eyes on the back of the house and there was no sign of anyone stirring. He was afraid to signal again, and he had waited long enough to escape censure later. He put the gun back across his shoulder and hurried along the alley. When he reached the edge of town a few minutes later the houses and the alley ended abruptly near a woods that stretched along a narrow bayou beside open fields of cotton. The street beyond the houses turned into a shady tree-lined road that led eventually to the next town several miles away. The woods at the end of the alley was his destination.

As he neared it, he neared also the end of his plan. He had not thought beyond that. Beyond reaching this point before everyone else was stirring, beyond getting to the woods unseen, secreting himself, and being there. That was as far ahead as he had let himself think. He had told himself, he supposed, that they would decide together, that beyond that point it would become *their* plan, that together they would decide what to do next. But in truth there had never been any plan.

A plan would have meant answering questions that he had never even asked himself, questions about what he thought he was doing, and why he was doing it in the first place. Questions to which, even if he had bothered to ask them, he would have had no answers because there were none. None that to him would have made any sense at least, just as none of the questions would have made any better sense, which was why he had never asked them. This was not about questions. It was about doing something he wanted to do, something he needed to do. A plan would have involved thinking it through, considering the consequences, weighing the possible outcomes, making judgments, the kind of judgments that at the outset would have meant he never would have considered doing it at all.

At some level he understood all of that without bothering, or being able, to articulate it exactly. He had simply bypassed this other process and all the questions that he would not have been able to think of anyway and to which he would have had no answers even if he had thought of them, and simply acted. Those actions that brought him to the edge of the woods had been his only plan, all the plan he had needed to successfully get him this far. And getting this far was what it had all been about.

Now at his destination he could not avoid thinking about what came next. And he didn't know, or want to confront the realization that he didn't know, that there was no plan, that the only plan of sorts had been the adventure itself. To this point the adventure had been reason enough for everything he had done to get here. But he couldn't stop the clock. Or the workings of that other everyday world out of which he had stepped, even if only for a brief time, in his furtive escape to the woods. And he couldn't undo what he had done. He could hear the first sounds of morning traffic in the distance. By now his family would be awake, and by now they must realize he was gone, with no idea about where or why. He had said or done nothing, except in his own thoughts, to make them suspect anything like this. He tried for an instant to picture the scene and their reaction but found that he couldn't and didn't want to. Perhaps they wouldn't care after all. That later he could return as casually as he had climbed out the window and left, without anyone considering it anything out of the ordinary. That was the outcome that he wished at that moment but realized was not possible. His parents' world was one where there were always consequences. He knew the time was fast approaching when his father would have to decide whether to leave for work as usual. He wondered what he would do. He didn't want to have to think about that either.

For now he put it out of his mind as he made his way deeper and deeper into the woods. When he reached the bank of the bayou he sat down beneath a tall yellow poplar. High overhead a yellow-shafted flicker called, moving from tree to tree and drumming loudly on the side of each. A band of blue jays moved raucously through the understory, drawing the stern scolding of a gray squirrel nearby. He watched until he spotted a red-winged blackbird where it called from its perch amidst a clump of cattails at the edge of the bayou. In the distance he could hear the sweet liquid notes of a cardinal repeated over and over and in the opposite direction the spirited banter of a mockingbird. Once or twice he heard the soft distinctive tapping of a sapsucker and the rattling peek of a downy or a hairy woodpecker. A small flock of chickadees worked its way methodically through the flowering dogwoods that grew interspersed beneath the taller poplars and hickory trees. From somewhere behind him came the flute-like call of a hermit thrush.

Except for its own sounds the woods were quiet. The thick vegetation dampened outside noises. The foliage diffused the morning light evenly and bathed the interior in soft cool shadows. It would be midmorning before the sun rose high enough for its light to penetrate the small clearings and open spaces that lay scattered through the woods. Until then the damp cool of early morning would linger, giving way gradually when it did to the muggy warmth of afternoon. In the clearings grew dense tangled thickets of cocklebur and brier and cane and honeysuckle vine. At times the entire woods reeked of the cloying fragrance of honeysuckle blossoms.

He sat, his back against the trunk of the towering poplar where he could see and hear in both directions along the bayou, and took in everything around him. He was guided as much by sound as by sight. Most of the birds he heard went unseen. Once he heard a faint crackling noise coming from a thicket downstream. When he looked again later he saw a doe and a smaller deer that he took to be a yearling fawn standing in the open beside the bayou where they had come to drink, quietly watching him. They finally caught his scent on the heavy humid air and bounded off, crashing through the dense thicket. They will drink farther downstream, he told himself, sorry that he had interrupted them.

He was not thinking about what he was going to do next. He thought only about what he was doing at this moment. It reminded him of why coming here had been the only plan, why he had not thought beyond that, beyond getting here and being here. This was where he most liked to be, where he went to get away from things for a while, to think about the present and the future and about all of the questions that his life up to now had caused him to wonder about but for which he had no answers. Here the questions never seemed to matter as much. This place was itself an answer of sorts if only because it brought the questions into perspective and made them seem less important, less urgent. Just being here reassured him that the questions would someday have answers even if he didn't yet know what they were. He knew that this place, this tiny woods stretching alongside a sluggish bayou between open cotton fields and a road that led from one town to the next and the next, in a countryside dotted by the remaining remnants of once vast forests now diminished to scattered woodlots by the encroachment of ever more towns and cotton fields, was not a destination but a beginning, a starting point. The pack, the shotgun, the quiet escape into the night and the furtive journey through the dark and early dawn to reach here unseen and undetected, to be here and to lose oneself for the moment in the sights and sounds of the trees and plants and birds and the knowledge he already had of them, the anticipation and mystery and excitement of it were all emblematic of a larger adventure on which, without even knowing what it might be, he already sensed he would someday embark never to turn back.

The sounds of dawn with its avian chorus gradually subsided and gave way to the quieter warmth and stillness of mid-morning. The last to go were the cheery greetings of a cardinal and the haunting flute sounds of a hermit thrush. Leaving the pack and the gun concealed in bushes near the poplar, he explored deeper into the woods downstream along the banks of the bayou. The stream was full of silvery minnows and he startled several bullfrogs sitting at the water's edge, but he saw no fish. He had hunted the bullfrogs at night with a light but he had never fished the stream. The only fish he had ever seen here were carp and were not considered good to eat. He found where the deer had gone down to the water to drink, leaving deep heart-shaped holes in the mud along the bank. In a small clearing beneath a hickory tree the ground was littered with the whitish droppings and dense regurgitated food pellets of a barred owl. The pellets were laced with the tiny bones of small rodents encased in their undigested fur and hair.

He wandered only far enough to examine his immediate surroundings and assure himself he was alone. When he returned he retrieved the pack and gun from the bushes and once again sat with his back against the yellow poplar. He studied the large thick tulip-shaped leaves high overhead. A few yellow and orange blossoms were still visible here and there amidst the thick foliage. It was for the shape of the leaves and the brilliant colorful blossoms that it was known locally as the tulip tree.

As he sat admiring them sweat slowly trickled down his

face. The heat was becoming sticky and drowsy. The scene around him gradually blurred into a fixed panorama in which he no longer noticed anything separately but only as patterns in a larger mosaic. Individual sounds faded from hearing into an indistinct hum of background noise. The loss of sleep the night before overtook him and he dozed off.

He awoke a few minutes later to the vague awareness of someone close by calling his name. He listened while he heard it again. He peered around the tree to see his sister approaching.

"Andy, Andy," she called. "Andy, where are you?"

"Here I am," he answered. He slowly stood up. "How did you find me?"

"Andy, where have you been? What do you think you're doing? You've got everyone all upset. You have made Mother cry."

"I haven't done anything," he tried to protest. "I've been right here. I didn't mean to make her cry."

"Well you *did*. I've never seen Mother cry like that before. It was awful."

"How did you know where I was?"

"Mother called Mrs. Greer trying to find you. And she made David tell what you had planned. He said you might be here. Where have you been? I've been calling at the top off my voice for half an hour."

"I've been right here the whole time. I didn't hear you until just now. I...I guess I fell asleep for a while."

"Well you better come home this minute. Mother is really upset. She's been crying and crying. You ought to be ashamed of yourself."

He was afraid to ask about his father. "I didn't do anything to intentionally upset her. I didn't intend to make her cry."

"What do you call running away from home? What did you think she would do? How did you think she was going to feel? What's gotten into you, Andy?"

"I'm not running away," he said. It was the first time he had spoken the words, the first time he had allowed himself to describe what he was doing in that way. He wasn't running away. He knew that. That was why there had been no plan for what to do, beyond what he had already done, beyond coming here and being here. If truly running away, beyond some fantasy of it in his mind, he would have had to plan what to do next and he had never taken that step or even allowed himself to think about what he was doing as running away. "I am not running away," he repeated.

"Well it certainly looks like it," she said. "What else would you call it?"

"I don't have to call it anything," he said. "It's just what I'm doing."

"Well you sneaked out of the house and slipped away without telling anyone. You know Mother and Daddy would never allow that. And you know Daddy would never let you take that gun out of the house by yourself. I don't know what he'll do when he finds out."

"You don't have to tell him," he said.

"He'll find out soon enough."

"Where is he?"

"He left for work after Mother talked to Mrs. Greer. Said he would be back later. You better get home before he does. You're in enough trouble as it is."

"You don't have to keep telling me."

"I'm trying to help you. Come home with me right now before you make things any worse."

"How did you get here? Did you walk?"

"I rode my bike. We could double up. You can ride back with me."

He thought for a moment. "No. I'll come home. But I want to go by myself, my own way. Anyway, we couldn't carry everything with the two of us on the bike. Tell Mother I'll be there as soon as I can."

"You promise, Andy? If I tell them I found you and didn't bring you back with me, I'll get in trouble too. Please, go with me. I'll tell them I met you on your way home."

"No. I promise. Just say I wouldn't go with you. That I'm on my way. It won't take me long to walk it. I'll be there shortly. Just tell Mother not to worry, that I'll come straight home."

"You better hurry. You've made enough trouble as it is."

He shouldered the knapsack and the gun and turned toward the way she had come. "Where did you leave your bike?" he asked.

"Beside the street at the edge of the woods," she said.

Instead of retracing his steps he veered to the right and followed the bayou to come out of the woods where the stream flowed under a bridge at the end of the street. There they found her bike. He turned back toward the alley as she rode away down the street.

"You better come straight home," she said before starting out.

"I will. I will," he answered. "Tell her I'll be there in just a few minutes." He stood for a moment and watched her ride off. She turned back once to look for him but he had already vanished into the edge of the woods. When she didn't see him she quickened her pedaling and was soon out of view.

He emerged from the woods and across a small open space into the alleyway. He walked fast but taking care to make as little noise as possible. He did not want to be noticed or draw attention to himself. He stopped every so often to listen for the sounds of people in the backyards on either side of the alley. Once he heard talking and he stood motionless until a back door slammed and the talking ceased, then hurried on. He carried the shotgun in his left hand, grasped around the middle, with his arm fully extended at his side, not over his shoulder as before, trying to keep the gun as much out of sight as he could. He felt exposed and self-conscious about carrying a shotgun, even an unloaded one, out in the open in plain view down the deserted alley in the middle of the morning. What had seemed all right under the cover of dawn now seemed uncomfortable and risky, even dangerous. He was not sure how he would respond if confronted other than simply walking on by as fast as he could. He saw no signs of anyone as he approached David's house for which he was grateful. He hurried past until he was well out of sight.

He had reached the halfway point home and he began to feel more at ease. The alleyway was obscured from view of the houses along it for the remainder of the way. He would only have to expose himself when he reached the point opposite his house. There he stood for a moment in the alley and listened to make sure he saw or heard no one, then slipped quickly between the houses and trotted across the street and through his yard and out of sight at the rear of the house.

He thought for a brief instant about climbing through the open window he had climbed out of, to postpone the inevitable confrontation, but it seemed to him somehow small and demeaning and a craven denial of what he had done, and he rejected the notion. Instead he walked straight through the back door into the kitchen where his mother stood looking at him. He could see that she had been crying and now she started sobbing again.

"Oh, Andy, Andy, why did you do this to me? Why didn't you tell someone? Whatever am I going to do with you?"

"I'm sorry," he said. "I didn't mean to upset you." He felt ashamed and embarrassed, for her as well as himself. The shotgun in his hand suddenly seemed an enormous and outrageous transgression and he was grateful when it went unmentioned. "I'm sorry," he quickly said again. "I don't know what else to say. I really didn't mean to hurt anyone. I'm very sorry."

She had stopped crying. "Andy, I don't know what to do with you. I'm just going to let your father deal with this. Go to your room and stay there. He'll talk to you when he gets home." She breathed a sigh of resignation and turned away.

"Yes, ma'am," he said. He knew that for now there was nothing more to say.

Once in his room he closed the door. Everything in the room was just as he had left it. He returned the shotgun to the back corner of the closet. And he carefully replaced the three shells he had removed from the full box and put it back on the closet shelf. He had not thought to eat any of the fruit or the sandwich from the knapsack and for now he simply put the knapsack on the floor of the closet. He would unpack it later.

He lay down on the bed and stared up at the blank ceiling. He was grateful to be in his room with the door closed, with the rest of the world excluded and held temporarily at bay. He didn't want to have to face anyone right now. He would have been content just staying here isolated from everyone and everything, but he knew that was not possible. The loneliness of his situation confronted him and intruded on his thoughts. He felt sorry for himself. He was scared and he dreaded having to face his father. More than anything he dreaded the wait without knowing what his punishment would be. He dreaded having to explain himself to his father when he couldn't even explain it to himself, having to answer the questions he knew he would be asked, the accusations. He had never been comfortable talking to his father, and he sensed that his father was just as uncomfortable talking to him. They never seemed to have anything to say to each other. He knew his father would have to punish him. He supposed he would get a whipping at least. Maybe if he were lucky that would be all, and after that things could get back to normal again. He dreaded waiting, not knowing. He just wanted to get it over with so he could stop thinking about it, so he could stop feeling lonely and isolated and could quit feeling sorry for himself. The dread of waiting was always worse than the punishment itself.

For serious offenses, a whipping was his father's usual method of punishment. His whippings were never administered in anger. They were done more as a matter of principle, as what he deemed the appropriate form of punishment for the offense at hand, than as any attempt to inflict pain or convey real anger. "This hurts me more than it does you, Andy," his father would always say before whipping him, and Andy had no reason to doubt that his father could be right. The whippings were never that painful and were over quickly. Still they were intimidating, even frightening. Having to confront his father's displeasure and censure in that fashion left him embarrassed for weeks afterward and made him feel small and humiliated and ashamed. And nothing was ever accomplished. All it did was to drive a wedge further between him and his father.

His father did not come home at noon. His mother left him in his room alone with the door closed. He lost track of the time. Twice the phone rang and he heard his mother talking without being able to hear anything of what was said. Then he heard her moving about the kitchen and heard her humming. She always hummed when she wanted to take her mind off something. For the rest of the afternoon she went about her work humming to herself. Even that tiny bit of normalcy raised his spirits. He cheered himself further by eating first the banana and then the peanut butter and jelly sandwich from the pack, after which he lapsed back into the dread of waiting for a judgment made increasingly ominous by its ever more immediate prospect. The lengthening shadows outside his window told him that it wouldn't be long before his father came home.

Then he heard the car in the driveway. It stopped beside his bedroom window short of the garage and he saw his father emerge and go toward the back door and heard him enter the kitchen. Still he did not come to Andy's room. Then he heard a soft knock at the door and his father entered the room. He eased the door shut behind him. Andy sat on the edge of the bed and looked down at the floor.

For a short while his father said nothing. To Andy it seemed an eternity. "Andy, son, you want to tell me what you thought you were doing this morning?"

"I don't know, I guess," Andy said without looking up.

"Well I don't know either, son. You scared your mother half to death. And you worried the both of us. We were concerned about you. We had no idea where you were, or what might have happened to you, or what was going on."

"I'm sorry," he said in a low voice.

"I'm sorry too, Andy, and I'm disappointed. I expected better than that from you. I can't imagine what you thought you were doing or why you would put us all through that."

Andy didn't answer but sat motionless, still looking down.

For a while his father was silent too.

"What *were* you thinking?"

"I don't know," he said.

"What made you pull a stunt like that?"

"I don't know," he said again. "I don't really have a reason. It's just something I thought of doing, I guess."

"There must have been some reason, son, to cause you to sneak off in the night like that. Haven't your mother and I always taken good care of you?"

"Yes, sir," he said, his voice trailing off, embarrassed for them both by the question.

"What's that?"

"Yes, sir," he said, louder this time.

"Why would you want to run away from home then? There has to be some reason."

"I wasn't running away," Andy said.

"You weren't running away?" his father asked.

"No, sir. I didn't think of it as running away. I knew I would come back. I didn't have anywhere to go."

"So what did you think you were doing, son, if you weren't running away from home?"

"I don't know," Andy said, "I...I really don't." He looked up at his father. "I can't explain it, I guess. I can't explain it to anyone because I can't explain it to myself. I'm sorry. I wasn't thinking about how it would affect everyone else. I didn't mean to upset you all. All I can say is, I'm sorry."

It was all he could say, all he would say. The real reasons, the deeper reasons, were not things he understood yet or could admit yet, even to himself, or more especially to himself, or put into coherent thoughts that were also as honest and candid as they were coherent. And even if he could have, he would not have been able to put them into words that he could speak to anyone else, especially his father. They were not words that could span the gulf between them. When he said he didn't know, he was telling the truth. Even if he had known why, it would not have been a truth he could have told to anyone else.

His father stood there quietly for a long time. Andy looked down again. The long silence made him more uncomfortable. He had expected a whipping and now he just wanted to go on and get it over with. He didn't want to have to face any more questions, to have to say anything else except that he was sorry.

Finally his father broke the silence. "I don't know what to say, Andy. I really don't. And I don't know what to do either. I really don't. I'm at a loss. What do you think we should do?"

"I don't know," Andy said.

"I don't know either, son. I just know I don't want this sort of thing to ever happen again."

"Yes, sir...I mean No, sir."

"Do you understand?"

"Yes, sir," Andy said. "Yes, sir."

His father stood beside the bed and again for a long time did not say anything. Andy did not look up. He stared at the floor in the fading light coming through the windows, and thought to himself, he really doesn't know what to do. He doesn't know what to say. He doesn't know, any more than I do, he thought, he doesn't know either. He had never seen his father at a loss, and it shocked and surprised him. He had never even considered that possibility. It surprised him, but it also alarmed him. His father's uncertainty added to Andy's burden. It was brought about by his actions, and he would have to face its consequences. A simple whipping would be so much quicker and easier, he thought. Instead, he didn't know what to expect.

"Do you mind if I sit down?" his father asked finally.

"No, sir," Andy said, and scooted over to make room beside him on the bed. His father sat down and stared at the bedroom wall straight ahead. Andy glanced at his father only to find that he seemed not to be looking at anything in particular.

"I ran away from home once," he said, in a flat expressionless voice, almost as if talking to himself. "Only I was a lot older than you. And I never went back. It hurt a lot of people, especially my mother. My father died years before. I was too young at the time to remember him. If she hadn't had all of my older brothers and sisters to think about, it probably would have killed her. As it was, it was bad enough." He looked over at Andy. "I wouldn't want to see you make that same mistake."

Andy didn't know what to say. Finally he just said, "No, sir."

He had never heard his father talk like this, to anyone, least of all to him. Andy sat in stunned silence. For the first time he confronted how little he might really know about his father, how different he might be from the way Andy had always imagined him and thought of him. "I didn't know that," he said at length.

"I know you didn't, son. There are a lot of things you don't know yet. There's no fault in that. The only fault is in not doing anything about them once you do know. Remember that and keep your eyes open."

"Yes, sir," he replied, "I will."

They sat there in silence for a while after that, until his father reached over and put his hand on Andy's knee, and said, "I want you to promise me you won't do anything like this again without coming to me first and talking about it. You understand?"

"Yes, sir," Andy said. "I promise. And I'm sorry."

"Don't be too quick to be sorry, Andy. Give some thought to what you're apologizing for. Otherwise it just might not mean a thing." Then he added, "I don't intend to say anything more about this. We'll just let it go at that. Now let's go and have some supper. Your mother worked all afternoon cooking it. We might as well all start getting used to having things back to normal."

"Yes, sir," Andy said.

That night his mother came in and kissed him good night. After she had gone he found himself crying and he couldn't stop. He wasn't sure why or what he was crying about. It just felt good to cry, and he finally cried himself to sleep. When he woke in the morning it was already light and he felt rested and refreshed. The world seemed brighter than it had in a long time.

A MATTER OF CONFIDENCE

Andy couldn't take his eyes off the big kid on the mound. Six foot five, well over two hundred pounds, big hands that made the baseball look tiny, long arms that released the ball so far up it seemed to be coming down at you from Heaven, and a fastball that was just plain scary as Hell. Andy didn't know what his breaking ball was like, but from what he could see if he could just control his fastball and was able to throw enough of them, he wasn't going to need a breaking ball or any other kind of pitch.

Andy watched as several batters in succession stepped back away from the pitch and out of the batter's box as they swung and failed to come anywhere near catching up to the fastball. Swinging like that the ball wouldn't get out of the infield even if they managed to hit it, he thought. It was one of the things his father had pointed out to him. "Stand in there when you swing," the coach yelled. "Keep your feet still. You can't hit nothin' dancing around like that."

Bob Randall, one of the other kids had told him. Andy didn't know him but he had heard about him. Randall was three grades ahead of Andy, and all during high school he had been this big and this good according to the stories Andy had heard. This was his senior year, and with every pitch he threw he was working hard as he could toward a college scholarship to play baseball somewhere. Andy watched as the next batter bailed out flat on his back in the dirt at the sight of a high inside fastball aimed too close to his head for comfort.

"C'mon now," the coach yelled from behind the fence. "Throw 'em over the plate. This is supposed to be batting practice. And slow 'em down a little. Nobody can practice hitting if they never hit the ball."

The big kid on the mound stepped off and nodded his head.

The next pitch came right down the middle, slow and fat, and was fouled off. But a few pitches later the speed was right back up to something Andy had never seen before and that made him really nervous to watch. Even right across the middle of the plate, this guy's fastball was intimidating.

Andy had played sandlot ball with the other kids in the neighborhood. They would divide up and choose sides and play on a field with the correct shape and number of bases, but with dimensions dictated by the size of whatever lot they happened to be playing on, usually one of the vacant lots in the neighborhood. That was the first thing he noticed. The high school baseball field looked enormous. He had never even been on a field that big. That was one of the things he noticed too about the big kid on the mound. His fastball still looked blazing fast even on a field this size. Somehow it didn't seem quite fair to have to face someone with that kind of physical prowess. But this was varsity baseball where everyone was lumped together and only those who were good enough got to play and be on the team.

That part of it at least didn't bother him at all. Organized team sports had never appealed strongly to Andy, whether football or baseball or basketball. He recognized that he was somewhat of a loner. He would much rather be off by himself, or with his brother or a friend, fishing or hunting or shooting his bow, when he was not in school. Football in the fall interfered with dove shooting and rabbit and squirrel hunting. Basketball meant he would miss duck hunting later on. In the spring, track and baseball got in the way of fly-fishing and turkey hunting and just getting out and exploring the woods when they were at their finest. Andy didn't hunt or fish out of any special passion for them, except that of being outdoors. At heart he was a naturalist and an adventurer. Among his earliest books were field guides to the birds and mammals and trees. He liked the natural world better than the social world, though he depended on the one to preserve the other. Someday, he feared, it no longer would. He preferred the old ways and traditions that he read about in books, though he had never experienced them himself. In his heart he was always on the side of the Indians against the forces of civilization that had killed all the game and pushed them off the land. He had been amused to read that Henry VIII at one time banned the playing of golf because it interfered with the practice of archery. He preferred the idea of hunting with his bow and arrow even if it meant his success would be limited. He wasn't interested in some new method or new gimmick just because it promised to enable him to kill more game or catch more fish. Not only was he a traditionalist but also a bit of a purist. There was something noble to him about preserving and holding on to the ways of the past. The relentless competition for more and more and better and better, along with the never-ending advance of more sophisticated and more effective technology, seemed to be leading in a direction that threatened everything he loved about the natural world. But he realized too it was more complicated than that. He preferred the bow and arrow to firearms, but he also wanted the finest bow and the best arrows that modern technology and understanding could provide.

Andy had decided to give baseball a try this year. He knew his father had never understood why he was reluctant to try out for the school teams when he became eligible. Together they listened to baseball games on the radio. His father would bring the radio outside on weekends while they worked in the yard or washed the car and turn up the volume so they could hear it from wherever they were and they would listen to an entire game, from the playing of the national anthem to the final out. He had actually learned quite a bit about the game from things his father pointed out to him while they listened. His father had never played organized sports either. It was from him that Andy had gotten his love of nature and the outdoors and acquired his knowledge of hunting and fishing. But he thought Andy should, and this year Andy had decided to give it a try and see what happened.

He had his own equipment. His father had given him an official Louisville Slugger bat made of gleaming white ash and a regulation-size fielder's glove while Andy was still too young and too small to handle either. The first ball his father threw him sailed over the webbing of the glove and hit him square in the forehead cutting a gash in his head and knocking him to the ground. It was a long time after that before Andy regained his confidence and lost his fear of the ball and finally learned to catch and bat as well as the other kids. In the meantime he discovered a passion for archery; and shooting the bow, which he learned to do well, took the place of baseball and other sports for which he had much less interest and less confidence.

It wasn't that he lacked all confidence. By reading books he taught himself to shoot a bow correctly in the manner of English target archery and the great archers of the past like Horace Ford, whose book on shooting was one that he read and pored over. At some point everything he had read and taught himself came together and he discovered the correct feel of a properly executed shot so that he could reproduce it time after time. He was able to regularly split a slender cane stuck upright in the ground at a distance of ten paces. He practiced shooting from a similar distance at a Quaker Oats box sat on a wooden fence, until he could hit not only the cylindrical box but the much smaller face of the smiling Quaker on the side every time. He became so certain of his ability that he even shot the box off the head of a kid in the neighborhood who foolishly agreed to be part of a stunt by which Andy intended to impress his friends. The stunt backfired. To the other kids the hero of the feat was not Andy but the boy who bravely let him shoot the box off his head. At that point Andy stopped trying to impress others and became satisfied by the knowledge of what he knew he could do.

Andy held his bat up and looked at it. He had brought it with him to this first practice, along with his glove, thinking to use it. The bat had hardly been used at all. It still looked practically new although he had occasionally hit fly balls with it. He could swing it all right and he was used to the feel of it. The other bats he had picked up out of the equipment bag and tried didn't feel nearly as comfortable to him and he decided to go with his own bat.

He watched as one after another the batters faced the big kid on the mound. He didn't appear to be slowing down but getting stronger. He seems to be throwing harder with every pitch, Andy thought. He had never seen anything like it. But he wasn't wild, and every time he started moving the ball out of the strike zone the coach yelled at him to throw it right down the middle. "I'm trying to conduct tryouts here," the coach shouted. "I want to find out whether anyone can hit the ball, not whether you can strike 'em all out. Just throw it across the middle, waist high. Pitching tryouts come later. Then you'll get a chance to show what you've got." And for a few pitches the big kid would slow down a little, until he couldn't resist throwing it by them again, and Andy would sit and watch him throw fastballs past batter after batter who couldn't catch up to them, and when they did, mostly fouled them off or popped them up or hit little dribbles that didn't get out of the infield.

"Can't anybody in this bunch hit a baseball?" the coach bellowed. "This is the kind of stuff you're going to see this year, people. I was hoping some baseball players were going to show up out here today." The more he goaded the more the big kid bore down and the harder he threw.

At some point no one stepped up to hit next.

"Okay, let's have the next batter," the coach shouted. "C'mon, people, this is supposed to be the best part of the game. If you don't want to do this, how do you expect to play baseball? Let's go. Who wants to hit next?"

Andy stood up. I might as well do this he thought. He picked up his bat and walked slowly to the plate. His heart was pounding and his chest felt tight so he made himself go slow and he took several deep breaths on the way to calm his nerves. He took his time stepping into the batter's box and getting the feel of where he was going to place his feet. He rotated each foot in turn side to side and dug into place. He didn't like the feel of his footing so he held out his left hand and stepped out. He stepped back in and scuffed his feet back and forth until he had a comfortable place scraped out for each foot. He knew enough to realize that the very back of the batter's box gave him the most time to see and react to a fastball, and that was where he set up. It was one of the things his father had pointed out as they listed to games on the radio. He took a couple of slow practice swings to relax then brought the bat back and held it cocked. He felt more at ease now and he was thinking calmly.

He avoided looking the pitcher in the eye. He concentrated instead on his right hand. He gave the pitcher his most passive, indifferent expression. He didn't want to appear to be challenging him, but completely disinterested and unconcerned. That way, Andy thought, no matter what happens he won't have the satisfaction of thinking he knows how or what I felt. He was still getting set mentally when the pitcher released the ball. It went by him before he was prepared to swing. He tried not to look surprised. He stepped out of the batter's box and took a couple of hard cuts before stepping back in and bringing the bat back.

This time he was ready. He started his swing by shifting his weight forward and stepping toward the mound the instant he saw the ball leave the pitcher's hand. It appeared to move toward the plate along a perfectly straight line. He saw nothing but the ball. His swing was intended to just meet the ball over the plate. He didn't try to swing as hard as he could but just to make contact. It all happened so quickly he didn't realize for a moment what had happened. He heard the crack of the bat. He felt almost nothing in his hands, but when he looked up to find the ball it was arcing high upward and growing smaller in the distance. The kid in centerfield stood rooted to the spot and turned and watched it sail over the fence. The whole thing had been so effortless and smooth that he wasn't certain for a moment he had actually hit it. He didn't show any emotion or act jubilant because he wasn't sure at first what had happened.

The coach came running over from the first base line.

"Son, what is your name?" he asked.

"Andy, sir, Andy Johnston," Andy replied.

"Why haven't I seen you out here before, Andy?"

"I haven't ever played before, Coach," Andy said.

"Tell me, do you think you can do that again?" the coach asked. He glanced out toward the fence.

Andy looked at him and thought for a while before answering. "No...No, sir, I don't think so," Andy replied. "Not like that anyway."

"Yeh," the coach said. "I was afraid of that."

The look of disappointment on his face was plainly evident.

That's all right, Andy thought to himself. I can live with that.

THREE LITTLE SAVAGES

The headlights split the darkness for a short distance ahead and forced it to the shoulders of the narrow gravel road, then swept it swiftly rearward past the sides of the car where it closed together again in a roiling cloud of dust behind the red glow of the taillights. The tires made a smooth tearing sound in the loose gravel, punctuated by the occasional loud clanking of rocks ricocheting off the underside of the car. He could feel the impact through his feet against the floor. The dense plume of dust trailed far behind the car and slowly spread out to blanket the road and coat the vegetation along both sides. The moon, nearing full, would not rise for a while yet. The temperature outside was already below freezing and it would dip even lower before morning. The interior of the car felt warm and drowsy and subdued the nervous excitement with which they had loaded their gear before setting out. They rode now in silence. He had heard nothing from the back seat since shortly before turning off the asphalt onto the gravel.

From his seat beside his father he could see everything appearing in the headlights. Around each curve the broad swath of light swept across the edge of fields bordering the road. He caught sight of the fleeting round reflections from the eyes of feeding deer. As the car neared the levee, acres of brown withering cotton stalks dangling a few tattered remnants of white gave way to pastures of alfalfa and groves of trees. He began to see more and more deer drawn from the big woods behind the levee by the fields of lush alfalfa.

At the base of the levee the car slowed to bump across the spaces between the iron rails of a cattle guard at a gap in the fence. A short distance later the headlights swung sharply to the right across the gently sloping side of the grass-covered levee and up a sloping incline. The car slowly whined its way to the top and then abruptly

106

to the left and immediately down another long incline in the opposite direction to the bottom on the other side. From there the track, no longer gravel but only bare dirt now and deeply rutted, passed through a thin sparse grove of cottonwoods to a lake, once part of the river itself, and a ramshackle fishing camp carelessly moored alongside its bank.

The levee was the final rampart: the last bastion separating the diminishing portion of land still surviving in some semblance of what it had once been on one side, and the vast unbroken expanse of cotton fields and farms and the scattered towns it had long since become on the other. Though still too immature to comprehend fully the numbing mediocrity and commonplace of the towns and settlements, for the boy and his two companions this place nevertheless had already begun to be the sanctuary that for the remainder of their lives they would need in some form and seek out in whatever form they found it. Behind the barricade of the levee the land still flooded each year as it had from time immemorial, ravaged by the transforming rampages of the mighty river as it overflowed its banks each spring and surged landward, to be finally confronted and confined only by the bulwark of the low earthen mound stretching a few miles from the river along both sides, all the way from St. Louis to New Orleans. The land renewed and nourished each year, by the rich burden of alluvial soil borne from the vast and remote reaches of an entire continent upstream and deposited every spring as tribute to its indomitable past by the ancient flood on its annual sojourn to the sea. Logged in the past and even now in places from time to time, the woods were still allowed to flourish as the principal, indeed the only, cash crop. During most of the year no one ventured far behind the levee, drawn only by an occasional illicit whiskey still and the few hunting and fishing camps secluded in the woods or isolated along the oxbow lakes that once had been the main channel of the river itself, now shifted in its course by the endless erosion of its constant meanderings. Except for a brief interval each hunting season it was still a place where one could wander over thousands of acres of unbroken woods and virtual wilderness without encountering a single person. And it lay just on the other side of the long narrow loop of lake appearing straight ahead as a dark formless void in the headlights as the car crept down to the edge of the water.

"You boys go get George's boat and bring it over here," his father said.

The boy and his brother each took a short wooden paddle

from the trunk of the car. Then the three boys made their way single file down a narrow rickety plank onto the old wooden riverboat that served as clubhouse and floating marina for the jumble of small fishing boats tied up around all sides of it. They untied a flat-bottomed boat and got in, using the paddles to push it free of the tangled mass of boats until they reached open water, then rowed to where the car sat facing the lake with its headlights still on. They pulled the boat ashore and turned it over to dump the water out, then righted it and slid it partway into the lake.

They loaded their gear, stowing everything on the raised slats in the bottom of the boat where it would stay dry. A large canvas bag stuffed with food and old pots and pans made a resounding clunk against the side of the cypress boat. The sound reverberated across the lake and was quickly swallowed by the cold black void. Sleeping bags packed with spare clothes were rolled into tight compact bundles and securely tied. Last to be loaded were three large leather quivers stuffed with arrows, and three wooden longbows. The boy's hands were becoming numb from the cold and he jammed them into his coat pockets for relief. Everything was loaded and secured and they were ready to shove off. His father switched off the headlights.

"Do you have everything you need?" he asked. "Look it over one last time before I leave. After that, you're on your own."

"We've got everything we could think of," the boy said. "Anything we don't have now we'll just have to do without."

"You going to be warm enough?"

"We can build a fire. We brought plenty of matches."

"You know where you're going to camp?"

"Yes sir," he said. "There's a pond not far from the lakeshore. We'll have water for boiling and drinking there."

"Think you can find your way in the dark? Do you have enough flashlights?"

"The moon will be up soon, maybe by the time we get across the lake. We can get there by moonlight if we have to. But we have flashlights. And extra batteries. We have the Coleman lantern too. We'll be all right."

He knew the questions were as much to give them confidence as to second guess their planning and preparations. His father had trained them very early to be responsible, and to think for themselves. The questions were just his way of reinforcing that before letting them set out on their own.

"You boys be careful now, you hear me? When you get across

the lake signal with your light three times and give a barred owl call to let me know everything is all right. I'll be back here at the same time three days from now. If you run into any trouble or need me for anything before then, check with Mike in the clubhouse. He can give me a call."

Looking back from the middle of the lake, the only light they could see was the one over the entrance at one end of the houseboat. This time of year the caretaker would likely be the only person aboard and there were no signs of anyone stirring. Mike was probably already in bed huddled against the cold. No one would even know they were there, once they were in the woods. When they reached the other side, he blinked his flashlight three times and gave his best imitation of a barred owl: a booming *hoohoo-hoohoo*; *hoohoo-hoohoooaw*. The sound carried easily across the lake, and in the distance an owl answered. Soon, he knew, owls would be nesting. In a minute they saw the car lights and watched as they drove slowly away through the trees until they saw them climb the side of the levee and disappear.

Suddenly he felt all alone, and standing there in the unbroken silence of the endless darkness, shivering from the cold, he realized they all did.

"Well, we better get going," he said.

They unloaded the boat and hid it back in the trees well above the water line. They couldn't afford to take any chances of it being gone when they returned, stranding them there. They were completely surrounded by water, the oxbow lake wrapping around all but a short section of land which bordered the main channel of the river where it joined to the lake at each end. Once the entire island had been a peninsula jutting from the land on the other side of the river. Then the Corps of Engineers dredged a channel across the narrow neck of the peninsula, Cypress Cutoff they called it, shortening the river channel and creating this island on the other side.

It took two trips to portage all of their gear to the campsite a mile away. A faint game trail led through a narrow strip of willows and poplars lining the lakeshore and across a long broad meadow that once was a sandbar along the old river bed but was now grown up in shrubs and grasses, and from there back into the woods on the far side where after a short distance it came to a large shallow pond fed by springs at the foot of a low wooded ridge. Crossing the meadow they heard several deer snort and bound off. By the second trip they were able to make their way with nothing more than the light of the moon to guide them. Not a breeze was stirring. The physical exertion warmed them. Only their fingers and toes remained cold by the time they had everything moved to camp.

They did not stop until the lantern was lit and hung nearby from a low tree branch and they had gathered a supply of dead wood from around the pond and had a bright fire going in the center of the campsite. The ground around the fire was soon cleared of debris and three low mounds of dried leaves were raked up to insulate the sleeping bags from the damp earth. They stored their food and cookware in the canvas bag and suspended it with sash cord high off the ground from a nearby tree. They had no tent. They knew it was not likely to rain this time of the year, especially with it so cold, and they relished sleeping unconfined out in the open under the stars. When everything was finally in order they crowded around the fire to boil a pot of pond water for hot chocolate and to fill their canteens for the morning, and sat quietly on a short section of downed log enjoying the results of their efforts and the anticipation of the adventure they were sure was ahead. For the moment they felt secure and cozy in their little camp. It was the first time they had allowed themselves to relax and feel confidence in their ability to actually accomplish what they had planned.

They had been planning it ever since the day they discovered the wild hogs.

That was six months ago, the summer before. That day the boy and his brother had rowed across the lake to explore the island, thinking to search for the giant pileated woodpeckers whose calls they had heard from the lakeshore and which they knew must inhabit the wooded ridges of the island. They took along their bows and a supply of blunt tipped arrows for shooting at stumps and bushes and clumps of grass or clods of dirt or any other target of convenience. It was a game they played, imagining they were hunting. The one who came closest to the intended target won. Roving it was called in archery, back even to the days of Robin Hood and the early traditions of English archery, and it was ideal practice for the kind of offhand shooting at unknown distances that one did in hunting with a bow. The boy and his brother had already been shooting for several years and they imagined being able to kill big game with their bows.

Then one shot that ricocheted off a tree and into the thick brush beyond was met with a loud, angry squeal, and a wild hog suddenly ran out of the tall grass where it had been rooting in the sandy soil. The boys watched in silence, transfixed, as it disappeared across the open meadow and into the woods beyond. They looked at each other. That was a wild hog, they both exclaimed.

After that the woodpeckers were quickly forgotten. They turned instead to carefully stalking each place where they imagined another wild hog might be. Soon they were discovering large shallow craters in the soft soil, recently excavated by hogs tearing up the ground in search of roots and tubers and grubs. In some cases the scattered soil was still damp. The extent of the destruction was surprising. Some of the excavations were several yards across and deep enough to conceal a large hog or even a small group of hogs. They realized from the abundance of sign that there must be a significant number of wild hogs on the island. After all, there were thousands of acres and they had covered only a tiny portion of it. And the hogs were captive here, surrounded on all sides by water too wide and deep for them to easily cross.

Before long they spotted several hogs in one of the shallow craters and stalked close enough to be able to hear their soft grunts as they shoveled about in the fresh soil. In spite of their poor eyesight, the hogs still somehow sensed them and bolted for the nearest trees. Any doubt about whether they were wild or not quickly vanished as they fled. As they watched them cross the open meadow the boys knew that they would return sometime to hunt them with broadhead arrows instead of blunts. Then, sheepishly, they realized that neither of them had even thought to try a shot at the hogs with their blunt arrows. It would have been fitting confirmation of their future intent. They saw no more wild hogs that day but plenty of fresh sign. Maybe there weren't as many as they had hoped, they thought, but there were some, and that was enough to excite their imaginations.

Part of the appeal lay in the realization that they were wild hogs. Wild boar was how they referred to them collectively. The designation carried with it a lure of adventure and excitement, even a suggestion of danger and a test of courage that other forms of hunting lacked. The boy learned in fact that they were actually feral hogs, originally placed on the island as a way of confining them and raising them without having to feed them. When the scheme proved too much trouble and unprofitable, they had been simply abandoned and allowed to roam free. Someone told him that had been over twenty years ago, and in the many generations born since then they had become a mongrel race of rangy, shaggy-coated animals with a reputation, deserved or not, for ferocity and aggressiveness. The boy thought the reputation was probably undeserved. From what he saw that first day he suspected he was right. Still the prospect of facing them with nothing more than a bow and arrow deepened the fascination and excitement and made the prospect of hunting them all the more appealing to their youthful imaginations.

The bows they had been shooting up to that point were all right for small game like rabbits and ground squirrels but for larger game they would need more powerful weapons. So they had to wait until they obtained stronger bows, almost at the limit of what they could handle with any consistency, and learned to shoot them, and until they had accumulated an adequate supply of arrows tipped with sharpened hunting points. Then they had to wait until after deer season in the fall, when there would be other hunters on the island, many of whom his father did not know and around which he did not want the boys hunting. Too many damned fools in the woods this time of the year, his father said. He allowed them almost complete freedom in the outdoors except where it meant being around other hunters whose judgment and actions he did not trust, which meant practically everyone else. It was his father's one concession to the concerns of his mother, who, the boy knew, except for his father's firm insistence, would have given them far less liberty than they actually enjoyed. It was precisely because his father was so adamant, he supposed, that his mother felt relieved of the responsibility, and any guilt over the consequences, and went along with whatever his father would allow.

In the meantime they recruited another boy who, like themselves, was a youthful romantic and shared their fascination with archery and hunting wild hogs with a bow and arrow. They often shot together. He was a year older than the boy and almost three years older than the boy's brother and was a resourceful and proven companion. To the boy the three of them seemed like the ideal number. Together they planned and schemed and saved and gradually acquired whatever they needed. Now at last they were on their own, seated comfortably around a campfire in the big woods behind the levee, in the middle of the night, on an island surrounded on every side but one by a lake filling the old river bed and on the other by the man-made channel of the ancient river. It was as close as they could get to imagining what the primeval wilderness that once stretched unbroken across this fertile swampy expanse of land had been like before people invaded it and drained it and cut it up for farms and roads and settlements.

112

The lantern was extinguished to conserve its fuel. The slowly diminishing fire illuminated only a small space immediately surrounding them, beyond which stretched a mostly formless void. Whenever they peered outward it was into an empty darkness that not even the moonlight could dispel. They sat for some time in silence, lost in thought, listening to the soft crackle of the fire.

Suddenly the silence was pierced by a tremulous whinnying, a high-pitched screeching that grew in intensity and seemed to emanate simultaneously from everywhere around them. They sat, momentarily paralyzed, too startled to move, unable to imagine what they were hearing or what it could possibly mean. The darkness and their isolation made the sound all the more frightening. Once started, the screeching persisted and seemed to come from everywhere, just beyond their fingertips. Then as suddenly as it had begun the sound abruptly ceased and the overwhelming silence of the night intruded once more. They sat without speaking, each of them wondering what the others were thinking, afraid and embarrassed to do anything that would reveal his own bewilderment.

Then as abruptly as it had stopped, the sound started again. Only this time its strangeness gave way to a growing realization that this sound too, so new and foreign at first, must be some natural phenomenon, and almost in unison the three of them exclaimed: a screech owl. Not one screech owl—which all of them knew about but which none had ever actually heard alone at night in the woods—but several screech owls calling in unison from the trees around them, perhaps attracted to the fire. The owls were beginning the process of establishing nesting territories in advance of mating later in the season.

Each of them sat quietly, suddenly relieved that he had done nothing to reveal his initial fright. Slowly conversation resumed and gradually each became aware that his own reaction only mirrored that of the others. The experience united them and brought them closer together. They had withstood the first test and emerged with their dignity and confidence intact. No one felt sleepy anymore. They built up the fire and sat discussing plans for the morning.

Eventually they lapsed once more into a passive silence and were contemplating crawling into their sleeping bags to escape the deepening cold when a second noise, this time farther off, brought them out of their reverie. Only now they were not frightened and realized at once what it was: the throaty, squealing rage of wild hogs fighting, boars contesting among themselves to mate with the sows, they guessed. This sound was not isolating but reassuring. Here was unmistakable proof that there were wild hogs nearby, and, from the sounds, several of them. The noise seemed to be coming from beyond the far end of the pond perhaps several hundred yards away. They listened, fascinated, to the primitive squeals of one boar being punished by another. It sounded like a fight to the death and lent instant credence to the reputation for ferocity and belligerence. Gradually they could distinguish in the distant melee what they imagined were the voices of several different individuals.

Their prospects for success suddenly took on new life. "This is our big chance," the boy said. "We can walk right up to them in the dark while they're fighting. We'll never have a better chance to get close enough for a really good shot."

In the time it took to slip on an arm guard and a shooting glove, then string their bows and sling a quiver over their shoulder, the three of them moved off through the trees toward the sounds of fighting. Once away from the fire their eyes adjusted to the dim shadows of the dense woods. They went quickly at first until they began to hear the fighting more clearly and realized they were getting close. They stopped at one point to nock an arrow and make final adjustments to their equipment. The fighting was much louder now. The hair began to stand up on the back of the boy's neck and he started to shake from excitement. He was breathing faster and he felt his heart racing. He tried to calm himself but that only seemed to call attention to his nervousness and made him shake more. He took a deep breath, then drew his bow as if to shoot; the tension in his muscles calmed him some. He made several more practice draws after which he felt back in control again. He was not frightened, merely excited. His only real fear was that he would not be able to make the shot when the time came, that at the crucial moment he might miss and disappoint himself and lose the chance they had worked and waited for so long. He tried to put that thought out of his mind but found it wasn't easy. He tried visualizing instead the act of shooting, of picking out and focusing on the spot to be hit and drawing and taking sure aim and releasing without thinking, the way he had practiced and trained himself to do. Forget everything but the shot, he told himself. It's going to be just like any other shot. Do everything the way you have practiced and the arrow will go right where you are looking, he assured himself, the way it always has.

Now that they were closer they tried moving more quietly but the thick carpet of dried leaves made that impossible. Yet nothing they did seemed to disturb the sounds of fighting. They crept cautiously forward from tree to tree until the sounds seemed to come from not one but several places spread out in front of them. They could now make out indistinct movements in the dark shadows. He guessed they must be within ten or twenty yards. Any closer and they risked spooking the hogs before they were ready to shoot.

In a low whisper the older boy, who was on the right, signaled he would turn on his light; the other two could shoot first. They slowly spread apart to have room to shoot unobstructed. Suddenly the light flashed on and there was a frantic swirling of wild hogs in and out of the trees in front of them. For a brief moment the boy saw one dark form stop broadside not fifteen yards away. He quickly raised his bow and shot. He watched as the arrow hit the shoulder but didn't seem to penetrate very far. The hog slewed about and ran directly away from him. He could see it for only an instant. He lost track of everything else in the confusing blur of movement and switched on his own light, trying to spot more hogs for the others to shoot at. They were quickly disappearing in the dark. The older boy shot at one but missed. His brother too had missed a shot at a running hog. There was no disgrace in that. A moving target in the excitement and dim light was a difficult shot, even at this close range.

All sounds of the fleeing hogs quickly died out. They switched off their lights and stood in silence, listening. Soon they could hear nothing at all. All evidence of the swirling commotion and confusion of a few moments before was now swallowed up by a dull empty silence.

"I hit one," the boy said, "but I don't know how bad it was hurt." They knew to wait, to give a wounded animal time to stop and lie down and bleed to death. After a short while they moved ahead to where the hog had been standing. There they found a few small drops of blood and began to slowly follow the faint blood trail. But after a few more yards they came upon the boy's arrow and there was blood on only the very front of the shaft. The arrow had pulled out of the wound, making it unlikely it had penetrated the rib cage. I must have hit the shoulder blade or the leg bone, he said. They could find no more blood beyond where they recovered the arrow, even after searching for several minutes in a widening arc. With no blood trail to guide them they had no idea in which direction to look, and finding the animal at night, even if it was mortally wounded, would be almost impossible. The boy couldn't hide his discouragement. To come so close and be denied, he thought. He had never imagined that if he hit one he would not kill it. To be able to get close enough to hit it had seemed the only problem. I would much rather have missed completely than to wound it and have it get away, he said. It could go for miles, the boy's brother told him. We would never be able to find it. Better to give up, or try again tomorrow if you think we should. Reluctantly they all agreed, and now cold and disappointed they returned to camp. They spent a few minutes more listening for sounds of hogs but heard none. At last they slipped into their sleeping bags and went to sleep.

The night was bitterly cold and the boy slept fitfully. The sleeping bag was too thin and light and was inadequate against the freezing temperature. He knew beforehand it would be, but it was all he had. His toes and fingers were numb and no matter how he lay or turned he could not get comfortable. At one point he awoke to the sounds of rustling in the leaves nearby. Turning on his flashlight he found a skunk only a few feet from the end of his sleeping bag, perhaps attracted by the warmth or by some scent. The skunk seemed oblivious to the light and continued scratching about in the leaves. He turned off the light and remained motionless and eventually the skunk wandered off. By dawn he was anxious to get up and build a fire and try to get warm again.

Morning came bright and sunny under clear skies and warming temperatures. A thick layer of frost coated the ground but the first rays of sunshine quickly melted holes in it and left the grass covered in a heavy dew. They fried bacon crisp and scrambled some eggs and ate them both with sliced bread buttered and toasted over the fire in an iron skillet. The hot food bolstered their spirits and brought back the excitement and enthusiasm of the evening before. After everything was cleaned and put away, they decided not to look for the wounded hog and made plans to hunt instead along the edges of the open meadow. There, they reasoned, they had the best odds of spotting the hogs first, then deciding how to go about getting close enough for a shot.

Emerging from the woods past the end of the pond they made their way carefully along the near side of the meadow. After going a few hundred yards they spied a large sow with a litter of half-grown shoats coming out of the woods more than two hundred yards ahead of them. The hogs were slowly feeding out onto the open meadow. Everywhere nearby the ground was pocked with craters, or wallows, where hogs had dug up the vegetation. The sow and her litter were wandering aimlessly from one crater to the next as they strayed farther from the woods. Eventually they settled down to feeding in one small area near the middle of the meadow. They were swallowed up and lost from sight in a large wallow. Every few minutes they would see the arched back of the sow or one of the shoats would wander out of the crater to another one nearby.

"I bet I could get close enough for a shot by crawling on my belly from one of those wallows to the next," the boy said. "If they spook before I get close enough, the two of you could intercept them where they came out of the woods. They'll probably go back in the same way they came out if I come at them from the other side. Or, one of you can make the stalk, and I'll stay along the woods."

"No, it's your idea, you make the stalk," his brother told him. "Only go slow and take your time. They aren't going anywhere. It's a lot easier to hit one of them while they're standing still than after they start running."

"Pick one of the shoats," the other boy added. "They'll make much better eating."

He waited until they were in position at the edge of the woods and had signaled him. Crouching low he headed straight across the open meadow toward the other side. He was far enough from the hogs that if he kept low and moved slowly they wouldn't be able to see him from there. Once he reached the other side he crept through the trees along the edge until he drew even with the hogs. Beyond them he could see where his brother and the other boy were waiting. The hogs were still more than two hundred yards away. He got down on his belly, and sliding his bow carefully along beside him, he headed directly for the group of wallows closest to the hogs. He moved only when he could no longer see any of the feeding hogs. Finally he reached the first depression large enough to conceal him and crawled into it for cover. From where he was he still couldn't see any of the hogs whenever they were down in one of the wallows. For the next few minutes he slithered as close to the ground as he could get, from one crater to the next, hiding in each one and peering over the edge of it until he was sure he could make it undetected to the next. His clothes were soaked with dew from the wet grass and the loose earth turned to soft mud and coated the front of him as he wriggled across each of the wallows. Sometimes he had to wait in a wallow for several minutes until all of the hogs were safely out of view. After more than thirty minutes of this he finally reached the crater closest to the one he knew the sow was in. There was nothing between him and his quarry now but a little more than twenty yards of open ground. There were no more hiding places. He had lost track of exactly where all of the shoats were. But he knew there would be no getting much closer without one of the hogs seeing him. From where he was he could hear them feeding and he knew they were still unaware of his presence.

He rested for a moment and thought about how to proceed. He finally decided that he would slowly rise up and, crouching, try to stalk as close as possible before shooting at the last moment when they finally sensed him. With any luck one of the shoats would be close by.

He stretched his cramped and aching muscles, took a few deep breaths, brushed the loose dirt from his bow hand and shooting glove, then nocked an arrow and got ready. He was up kneeling on one knee now and still no sign they knew he was there. Before standing he adjusted his quiver so that he could draw another arrow quickly if necessary. Then he rose up just high enough to keep the bottom limb of his bow clear of the ground and moved deliberately but carefully toward the wallow where the sow was feeding. As luck would have it she had her back to him and he managed to get several yards closer before one of the half-grown shoats came up out of the crater alongside and stood looking directly at him. Before he could get the bow fully drawn and shoot, the shoat turned and ran and the arrow went well behind him.

He frantically snatched another shaft from the quiver and chased after the shoat, quickly closing the gap between them. As he did, he saw the sow come dashing out of the far side of the wallow, and the other shoats scattered in all directions. He slid to a stop, picked the nearest one, and shot again. Again he missed, this time aiming too far ahead. Two shots at less than fifteen yards, he thought, and he had missed them both. He thought he could probably outrun one of the half-grown hogs, but by the time he caught up to it he would be too winded and excited to shoot steadily.

Instead he drew another arrow and came to a complete stop. Suddenly everything around him slowed too. He was no longer even aware of the shoats. He noticed only the isolated image of the tall, long-legged sow, still running, but seeming to be moving now as if in slow motion, straight away from him. Everything but that single moving form was shut out of his view. Without hesitation or conscious thought he raised his bow and drew it in one smooth, steady motion until the only other thing he saw was his arrow poised along the path that in his mind he imagined watching the streaking arrow follow in order to converge in the distance with the moving object. With no discernible pause he released, his drawing hand continuing backwards. He heard the soft hissing sound of the long low feathers and saw the gleaming cedar shaft arcing upward in the morning sunlight along the path he had pictured in his mind, then, watching still in his mind, saw the graceful shaft swooping swiftly earthward once more to fatefully converge with the fleeing image of the sow. The hog suddenly pitched forward and plowed to a stop in the freshly rooted earth, its spine neatly severed at the shoulders. At once he heard the whoops and shouts of his two companions, and then the jubilation of all three as they rushed wildly to claim their prize and danced gleefully, joyfully around their trophy.

On the evening of the last day they waited in the growing darkness at the edge of the lake. All of their gear was once more carefully stowed in the bottom of the boat. In the shallow front end were piled three wild hogs, all neatly field dressed. The older boy had killed one of them, and his brother had killed two more. One of the latter, smaller than the others, they had already skinned and cut up and roasted over the fire and eaten. They weren't the fierce, savage creatures that in their youthful dreams they had wanted to imagine, but they knew in their own minds they had nevertheless accomplished a feat worthy of themselves. They felt a not unreasonable pride and relaxed in the warm reverie of a satisfied silence. They would wait here in the dark until they saw their father's headlights. Then they would row in grand triumph across the lake. Wouldn't their father be surprised, and pleased, the boy told himself. Then, much later, maybe I will be able to write about it, he thought.

A MATTER OF LUCK

The jeep was almost on them before Andy ever saw it. His first impulse was to run for the woods but he quickly thought better of it.

"Where did that jeep come from?" he said.

"I don't know," Andy's brother said. "I never even heard it."

"I still don't hear it," Andy said. "That's got to be the quietest jeep ever."

He never imagined that anyone could drive up behind them out in the open like that without either of them seeing or hearing anything. Otherwise they would not have gotten so far away from the woods. They had been on the island for three days and in all that time they had seen or heard no sign of anyone.

The wide grassy sandbar they were walking along stretched between dense woods on both sides. An old jeep trail ran down the middle of it. They walked along it looking for signs of wild hogs that came out of the woods to root for grubs and tubers in the soft sandy soil. The sandbar had once been part of the riverbed. Then years ago the Corps of Engineers cut a new channel across the narrow neck of land formed by a long loop of the river in its constant meanderings, and shifted its course several miles to the west. An oxbow lake, still connected to the river at both ends during high water, was left where the old river channel had been. The island lay stranded between the lake on three sides and the new channel far to the west on the other.

"What are we going to do?" his brother asked.

"There's nothing we *can* do now. We'd never make it to the woods from here before they caught up with us. The only thing to do is keep walking and act like nothing is wrong."

As the jeep neared them Andy moved off the trail and turned to face the vehicle. In it he saw four men, none of whom he could

120

remember ever having seen before. The jeep slowed and came to a stop beside them. Andy rested the bottom end of his strung bow on the ground and leaned nonchalantly against it as a prop. The driver switched off the engine with hardly any noticeable change in the sound. That's the quietest jeep, Andy thought to himself. For a few moments no one spoke. Then, "What are you boys doing?" the driver of the jeep asked.

"Nothing," Andy said. "Just exploring."

"Just exploring, you say."

"Yes, sir," Andy said. "Just hiking and seeing what we can see."

"Do you know who I am, son?" the man asked.

"No, sir," Andy said. "I guess I don't."

"I'm Hamilton Russell. I hold the lease on all of this land. And you boys are trespassing. This is posted property. The gentleman beside me here is head of the state game and fish department. The two gentlemen in the back are a senator in the state legislature and a state game warden. He pointed to the two men in turn.

"Yes, sir," Andy said. "We're glad to meet you."

"How did you boys get here?" the driver asked.

"We rowed across the lake," Andy's brother said. "Our father belongs to the fishing and outing club on the other side. The one with the old riverboat as a clubhouse."

"Did you know you crossed the state line when you did that?" the man asked.

"No, sir," Andy said. "We're still on the same side of the river." He did know it, but he didn't see any advantage in admitting that now.

"That makes no difference, son. Before it changed course the river used to flow right through here. Not only are you boys trespassing on posted property, you're in the wrong state as well."

Andy did not respond to that and for a while no one spoke. The men just sat and looked at the boys. Andy didn't know what to expect next, but he decided to just wait and take his chances.

"You seen any game?" the man seated beside the driver asked.

"We've seen a few deer, mostly does," Andy said. "There are wild hogs too. Lots of them. They can really tear up the ground where they root it up looking for something to eat. That's probably why we never see that many wild turkeys. The hogs tear up the nests and eat all the eggs. We have seen a few turkeys though."

The man turned to the driver. "Hamilton, I told you you're

gonna have to get those hogs under control if we ever expect to have any turkeys in here. You need to have your deer hunters shoot 'em on sight. Kill as many as they want. Kill 'em all for that matter. They're not protected. I'd let people in here year 'round to hunt 'em if I was you."

"Can't trust 'em not to shoot the deer out of season," the driver said.

"Yeah, I suppose," the man said. "But we need to get rid of 'em. You'd end up with a lot more deer too."

"My brother and I come here mostly to look at birds," Andy said.

"What kind of birds?" the senator asked, suddenly interested.

"All kinds," Andy said. "Woodpeckers are one of our favorites though. This is the kind of woods with lots of old dead trees that woodpeckers really like. All of the species native to this area are found here. Yellow-hammer, hairy, downy, sapsuckers, red-headed, red-bellied. It's the only place we've been that has lots of pileated woodpeckers."

"What's a—how do you say it—pileated woodpecker?" the senator asked.

"It's a large spectacular bird, about the size of a crow, with striking black and white markings and a brilliant red crest, and a startling majestic call that you can hear for a mile or more." Andy took a well-used and worn Peterson field guide to the birds from the pocket of his jacket. "Here, I'll show you." He turned to the section on woodpeckers and handed the book to the senator, pointing to the pileated woodpecker. The senator studied the illustration carefully and read the entry. He looked up from the book.

"The only thing like it was the ivory bill woodpecker," Andy said. "Even larger, with very similar markings and a band of white on the rear of its wings, and a long ivory-colored bill, but a call not as majestic, more like a tin horn tooting. The 'Lord God Almighty bird' the old-timers used to call it."

"I don't see them in the book," the senator said. He thumbed through several pages.

"They're thought to be extinct now. But actually no one knows for sure. The last one photographed was not all that far from here, on the other side of the river," Andy said. "We keep our eyes open for them when we're exploring. Who knows, they might still be around here somewhere in these secluded woods behind the levee. They need a lot of room."

122

"Did you know about any of this, Phil?" the senator asked the man beside the driver.

"Birds have never been my specialty," the man said. "'Lord God Almighty bird'. Where did you get that, kid?"

"I read it the first time in William Faulkner," Andy said. "I don't remember exactly where. I've seen it other places since then though."

"So, what you're saying is this place is unique, or at least unusual," the senator said.

"It's the only place we've found this many pileated woodpeckers," Andy said. "And there are lots of different kinds of birds too. This place has a number of distinct habitats. Dense woods, swamps and marshes, clearings, meadows and open fields, streams and ponds. It attracts a wide variety of species."

"Phil, this is exactly the kind of thing I was talking about, that we can use to get more funds out of the legislature. Hire additional staff for your department and put more resources into habitat protection and game management. There's something in it for everyone." He handed the book back to Andy. "I assume your hunting club wouldn't object to having some of those funds, would it, Hamilton?"

"I'm all in favor, long as we retain the hunting rights," the driver of the jeep said.

"You'd do better than that," the senator said. "When it comes time to renew the lease you could point to improvements in the property to strengthen your application."

"I suppose it couldn't hurt none," the other man said.

"That's right," the senator said. "'Lord God Almighty bird.' Almost like having our own Bigfoot. I surely would like to see one someday. What you're telling us is on the level isn't it, son?"

"Yes, sir," Andy said. "You can look it up. The last ivory bill ever photographed in the wild was not that far from here, and not that long ago, on your side of the river."

The men turned their attention from the two boys and for a few moments talked in hushed tones among themselves. The driver of the jeep and the man beside the senator in the back seat, who up to now had said nothing, did most of the talking. Then the driver turned to the boys and said, "You boys realize you're hunting out of season, don't you, I mean besides being on posted land and in the wrong state?"

"We're not hunting," Andy said.

"What are you doing with those bows and arrows then?" the man asked.

"Roving," Andy said. "At least that's what it's called in archery. It's a kind of game that archers play. We take our bows with us when we go exploring and practice shooting at whatever targets present themselves, a clump of grass, a bush, a stump, a mound of dirt, anything. You have to specify the target before you shoot, and the one who comes closest wins. It's good practice for hunting."

"Let's see one of your arrows," the man said.

Andy hesitated. There were two kinds of arrows in the leather quiver on his back, identical except for the type of point on the end. Roughly half of the shafts were tipped with razor-sharp broadheads, the kind of point used only for hunting. Andy had honed them with a fine-toothed file to an edge that would shave the hair off his arm. The other half were tipped with blunts, little metal cylinders flat on the end, the type of point used in roving to shoot at stumps and bushes and clumps of dirt or grass. The arrows with blunts were a couple of inches shorter than those with broadheads. But the arrows rode up in the wide leather case flattened against his back and protruded all manner of lengths from the mouth of the quiver. The ones protruding farthest were not always the longest and those protruding least not always the shortest. Andy knew that even by choosing one of the shafts not protruding as far, he still had no better than a fifty-fifty chance of pulling out a blunt. And he would have to do it by feel since even by looking over his shoulder he could not see how far the shafts stuck out of the quiver.

He reached back and placed his outstretched hand over the ends of the arrows and unobtrusively pushed them down into the quiver as far as he could, then by feel he grasped the nock on one that felt shorter than the others and pulled it from the quiver. He breathed a sigh of relief. It was tipped with a blunt point.

"It doesn't have a point on it," the man said.

"These are blunts," Andy said. "They're the kind of points we use for practice. They don't bury into things."

"Can you hit anything with those bows and arrows?" the man beside the driver asked.

"Sometimes," Andy said. Then pointing to his brother, he added, "He's a lot better than I am."

"Let's see you hit this hat," the man said, taking off the narrow-brimmed Stetson he wore and making a motion as if to throw it up in the air.

Andy handed the blunt-tipped shaft to his brother who quickly placed the arrow across his bow and nocked it on the string. The man tossed the hat straight up in the air. In one smooth easy motion Andy's brother canted the wooden longbow and drew it the full length of the arrow, until his right forefinger touched the corner of his mouth, and released the string. The arrow, streaking upward in the bright sunlight, converged with the hat at the top of its trajectory and tore a jagged gaping hole through the center of the crown. The hat, deflected sideways, fluttered back to earth beside the jeep. The arrow, barely slowed, continued its arcing trajectory and stuck upright in the soft ground sixty or seventy yards away.

"Damn you, kid," the man said. "You just ruined my best hat. I didn't mean for you to hit it." Andy hurried over and retrieved the man's hat and handed it to him. The other men laughed.

"You asked for it, Phil," the senator said, laughing, leaning forward and sticking his finger through the hole in the ruined hat. "Robin Hood and the 'Lord God Almighty bird,' and all in the same day. You got to admit," he said, "it's more in one day than anybody could have anticipated."

No matter what happened next, Andy thought, he felt good. He was proud of his brother. He had showed them all right. It was the kind of shot he had seen him make time after time, under pressure, when it counted. Maybe now at least they would take them seriously.

When the men stopped laughing and needling Phil, their attention turned once more to Andy and his brother. This time there was a different tone. The man beside the driver and the one sitting beside the senator conferred for a few moments. "Hamilton, do you want to prosecute these boys for trespassing?" the man beside the driver asked. "As far as I can see they haven't really broken any game laws. Being in the field with a weapon constitutes hunting, during a regularly scheduled hunting season. But there isn't any season open right now. Since technically they aren't hunting, it doesn't much matter what state they're in. I guess you can pretty much practice anywhere you want. They are trespassing however. By the way, I don't remember seeing any "posted, no trespassing" signs, if anyone were to try to make an issue of it. But trespassing is a matter for the county sheriff, not the game department. We'd have to take 'em back across the river with us. They're both minors. It'll upset their parents of course. It's your call."

"I don't want to fool with all that," the driver said. "I've got friends at that clubhouse across the lake. They help us out some during deer season. I don't need to get 'em all upset over nothin'. I'm satisfied if they just get off the property." He turned to Andy and his brother. "Where did you boys leave your boat?" he asked.

"About a mile or so ahead. Not far from where the road veers off toward the lake," Andy said.

"Well you boys go there now and get off the island before I change my mind. And don't come back over here, you understand?"

"Yes, sir," Andy said.

"Let's go," the man said and turned the jeep around in a large semicircle and drove off the way they had come. Andy and his brother walked slowly over to retrieve the arrow and kept their eyes fixed on the jeep until it turned off on a branch of the road that led up toward the woods.

"C'mon," Andy said. "They're going to go right past our camp."

That portion of the road wound along the ridge that ran through the center of the island, and after several miles it looked down on the large pond where they had made their camp. The camp lay in the open beside the pond and in plain sight from the road. The boys broke into a trot and kept it up until almost to the pond. The last few hundred yards they approached the pond cautiously through the woods. When they finally reached their camp everything was just as they had left it that morning. In a tree at the edge of camp hung the field-dressed carcasses of three recently killed wild hogs.

"We've got to get those hogs out of sight," Andy said.

They hurriedly cut down the hogs and covered them over with some of the dry leaves they had piled up to put their sleeping bags on. That done they rolled up the sleeping bags and tied them securely, shoved the cookware and the rest of their gear into a large canvas bag and put everything out of sight in the bushes at the edge of the woods. They took a stick and brushed the leaves out evenly to erase all traces of any disturbance, then hid in the bushes themselves where they could watch the road without being seen. They didn't have to wait long before they saw the jeep go by on the road above camp. It did not slow. They could hear the men talking, and they did not appear to be looking around at anything. They watched until the jeep disappeared from view in the trees at the far end of the long pond. The road led in that direction to the river at the other end of the island.

"They're probably headed back across the river," Andy said.

"I hope they stay there. C'mon, let's get out of here before our luck changes again."

It took four trips to get everything back to the lake and loaded in the boat. They took the hogs and their bows and arrows first, as the possessions they would least like to surrender. When the boat was finally loaded they sat down to wait. It would be getting dark soon. Their father was scheduled to pick them up on the other side shortly after dark. That way there would be fewer questions to answer. Will he ever be surprised to see these hogs, Andy thought. His father knew there were wild hogs on the island. He had seen them off three nights ago, with a caution to be careful and not to wander far from the lake. It wasn't hunting season. The island would normally be deserted. Andy knew his father never expected them to kill anything, not with bows and arrows, certainly not anything as formidable as a wild hog, Andy thought. But he didn't mind if they played at trying. He will be truly surprised, he told himself.

As they rowed across the lake, Andy's brother said, "Boy, luck was certainly with us today."

"I don't know," Andy said. "Getting caught out there in the open like that was pretty unlucky. And we just got kicked out of paradise."

"That was one thing. But when you pulled that arrow out of your quiver I thought the jig was up for sure. I just knew it was going to be a broadhead, one with dried blood all over it. We would have had a lot of explaining to do."

"I guess we *were* lucky, though," Andy said, "that we had the bird book and binoculars with us. And lucky too that senator fellow was along and was interested in something else besides what we were up to. That's one time that knowledge about something paid off."

"I'll take a little luck over knowledge any day," his brother said.

"We still got kicked out of paradise," Andy said. "That shot you made wasn't luck, though. Did you see the look on their faces when that arrow went through his hat? That was worth every minute of it." Andy and his brother laughed out loud. You could hear them in the dark all the way across the lake.

A DIFFERENT WORLD

The truck jerked to a stop. The four-wheel drive won't shift into low range with the vehicle moving, his brother explained. He clicked the gear shift lever smoothly into place and the truck lurched forward again. Now with the engine racing and the gears of the transfer case softly whining they slowly crawled and bounced their way up the narrow, deeply rutted track to a small clearing at the top of the ridge.

"We must be getting soft," he told his brother. "When we were younger we would have just hiked to the top."

"It's a different world now," his brother replied.

From here they could see in all directions. Behind them, the way they had come up, he looked back on the neat, close-cropped fields grazed by a flock of Dorset sheep. Beyond stretched a portion of the road leading from Meeker to Rifle. Adjacent to it, parked beside a small clump of cottonwoods near some old sheep pens, stood the little enclosed wagon in which the Basque sheepherder lived. Nearby, hobbled, two sorrel draft horses grazed nonchalantly. The Basque had told them about the trail to the top.

He watched one of the large Anatolian shepherd dogs lurking at the edge of the flock. They aren't herders, the Basque had explained. They were there to protect the flock from predators, mostly coyotes and mountain lions. They made him nervous whenever he was around them. The Basque warned them to stay clear of the dogs. They aren't dangerous, he said, only protective, and indifferent. They think they are sheep, not dogs, he smiled. When the sheep get nervous the dogs react. They stayed right with the flock all the time, day and night, good weather and bad, even when the Basque took food to them. What a strange solitary life, he found himself thinking. And it showed. Whenever they were around, it was clear that the

Basque craved company. He would do this only for a few years, he had told them. Then he would go back to his homeland in Spain. Still, he half envied the man his simpler life, close to the earth. He grapples with the only things that really matter, he thought, even the isolation and solitude.

In every direction stretched broad mesas and wooded ridges separated by flat-bottomed canyons running both east and west and north and south. In the bottoms of the canyons grew tall cottonwoods and ponderosa pines and on the sloping sides low thickets of gambel oak mixed with serviceberry and buckthorn. Higher on the ridges and at the upper ends of the canyons were scattered groves of aspen and darker patches of conifers, mostly fir; black timber the Basque had called it. In the clearings and meadows among the trees grew low shrubs and native grasses nourished by the winter snows and summer thunderstorms. In some of the canyons could be found small springs and wet areas. It was the grass and the water that lured the elk from the trees and brought them out into the open.

Looking immediately in front of them, to the east, he peered down into the broad mouths of three canyons separated by two wooded ridges running east and west and rising gradually in the distance to finally merge with a still higher ridge running north and south, parallel to the one they were on. The canyon bottoms were open and grassy in places, and the Basque had assured them that if they looked they would be able to find water. He himself had seen several large bulls out on the ridges, up by the black timber, he told them.

The man returned to the truck and came back with a long flexible tube partially closed at one end by a flat mouthpiece with a hole in the center across half of which stretched a thin rubber membrane. Peering over the edge of the ridge and pointing the open end of the tube outward, he put his lips against the diaphragm and blew a long, rising, high-pitched squeal ending in three deep throaty grunts. Almost immediately came a response, higher pitched still and fainter, but unmistakable.

"There's one out there," his brother said.

They stood for a while and searched the mouths of the canyons and the ridges between, his brother with a pair of small binoculars and he with his unaided eyes. He kept watching intently, expecting to see something move. "I don't know how well the sound carries," he remarked after a while, "but if he is standing in any of those dense trees he could be a lot closer than he sounds." He waited, hoping to hear a second bugle. Sometimes, this early in the fall, he knew that some bulls acted almost as if frightened by the bugling, especially the smaller satellite males still wary of the larger bulls. He had seen and heard them actually bolt and run away from the sounds of bugling nearby. But this time he hadn't seen any movement.

"Try it again," his brother said. He blew an even longer, louder whistle and let the grunts at the end taper off more gradually. This time there was no response. They stood listening for several minutes to make sure. Then they waited several minutes more to assure themselves the bull was not sneaking up the ridge toward them from below, where they wouldn't be able to see him. "Looks like we'll have to go down after him," his brother said. "It's still early in the afternoon. We've got plenty of daylight left."

Just as he was about to turn and go back to the truck, he took one last look over the edge into the canyons below. There to his right front he saw a bull elk emerge from the trees and cautiously cross an opening at the mouth of one of the canyons. The elk kept his head lowered and extended well forward.

"There he is, sneaking away," he said. The elk made it into the trees on the other side before his brother could spot him.

"How big was he?" his brother asked.

"He had nice symmetrical antlers. It was too far to tell how many points, but I would guess he was probably a six by six. Who knows if it was even the same elk," he added.

"Well, it looks like this is the right place anyway," his brother said. "All the signs are good. Let's hike down in there. The truck can't take us any farther. We have to be quiet from here on."

They returned to the truck and strapped on fanny packs. In each there were binoculars, an elk call, a skinning knife, a whetstone, some rope, and a full water bottle. Anything else they might need later they would leave here at the truck for now.

Their clothing was all camouflage, even to the fanny packs. Camouflage netting sewn into the rim of their hats covered their face and neck. Only their hands and the bows they carried were not cloaked in camouflage, and even they by contrast seemed merely another piece of the jumble of broken patterns and dull earth tones that covered the rest of them. Their bows were take-down recurves, with the latest, most advanced composite limbs made of wood and fiberglass and carbon laminates. They drew evenly and smoothly and felt even easier to pull than their fifty-five-pound draw weight and shot five hundred grain hunting arrows almost two hundred feet per second. To the handle was fastened the light frame of a bow quiver carrying eight aluminum hunting arrows fletched with plastic vanes. The smooth contoured grip of the handle was shaped to fit the hand. These were the crowning achievement of modern technology and the traditional bowyer's art, and a far cry from the simple wooden longbows and cedar shafts that he remembered from his youth. Yes, it is a different world now, he thought, recalling his brother's comment earlier. When we were boys, he reminded himself, all of this would have seemed foreign and unnecessary, even unwanted, some kind of cheating almost. Everything was much simpler then. All we needed was a plain longbow, strong enough, and a few straight arrows, reasonably well matched. After that, everything was up to us. I think it was much better in some ways, he uttered out loud.

"What's that?" his brother asked.

"Oh nothing," he said. "I was just thinking out loud."

Still, he had no real desire to turn the clock back. He had his memories, and what had been done was now done and in the past, and he was content to leave it that way. These newer bows and arrows were a joy to behold and a genuine pleasure to shoot, and it was the enjoyment and challenge of shooting well that appealed most to him. Yet he was willing to go only so far to make things easier, and he drew the line here.

The track they had followed to the top of the ridge now took them down the other side. The trail was bare dirt for the most part and the walking was fairly quiet and they went rapidly at first. In only a few minutes they had reached the first trees at the bottom. There they slowed and began looking well ahead before moving into any open spaces. It was nearing mid-afternoon and the woods was mostly quiet. Only a few sparrows and juncos and other small birds flitted around the edges of the clearings. Normally they would have stopped to identify some of them but they stayed focused instead on what brought them here. They did not want to miss seeing an elk by becoming preoccupied with birds that they could see any other time.

The mouth of the first canyon they hadn't been able to see well from the top of the ridge, and they now found that it was brushy and overgrown near the entrance and had thick trees farther in and few clearings. Reasonably wide at the beginning, it quickly narrowed. They went into it only a short distance before concluding there was not enough good elk habitat. The entrances to the other two canyons were connected by a long narrow glade grown up in bushes and tall grass and paralleling the ridge above. From there they could see a short way into each canyon. Both appeared to be pretty much the same. At the base of the ridge separating the two was where he had last seen the elk as it entered the trees. They had no reason to believe one held any better prospects than the other, and his brother arbitrarily elected to explore the middle canyon. They agreed to meet back here shortly after sunset, since after that darkness would come rapidly in these canyons, and his brother started slowly making his way into the cover of the canyon.

He continued on to the last canyon and was soon at the beginning of a long meadow of short grasses in which, farther ahead, he could see a darker green stain that he imagined might be rushes and thicker grasses. That could indicate water he thought. There was no appreciable cover in the meadow, which curved gently out of sight to the right well ahead of him so that he could see only a limited distance. The only movement of air he could feel was up the walls of the canyon. As the air cooled later he knew it would spill down the canyon toward him. He moved over to the base of the ridge that formed the near side of the canyon and eased his way carefully through the few trees and bushes at the edge of the clearing, so as not to be caught unawares out in the open.

It was a warm pleasant afternoon, and now that he was alone and unhurried he relaxed and took his time and allowed himself to enjoy the slight tingling sensation of nervous anticipation and animal excitement that always came over him when he was hunting by himself in an unfamiliar place. His imagination would conjure up situations that could conceivably arise in each set of circumstances he encountered, the prospects of which would heighten his awareness and put him pleasantly on edge. This was why he still hunted, not for the kill, but for the interest and excitement of the chase. He simply liked being here, immersed in the natural world around him, without all of the artificial constraints and considerations imposed by the necessities and contingencies of society. He no longer cared much whether he killed anything or not. What he craved was the feeling of excitement, the realization of still being able to, of being in the outdoors on his own, dependent on his own wiles and resources, and of doing everything properly that would finally give him an opportunity, without concerning himself about whether he ultimately succeeded or not. In his mind there was always a next time. He felt a sense of honor and an ethics about it now that he had never known to the same degree when he was younger. Back then, it would only have interfered with being successful, he guessed.

He began now to try to take in every small detail of his surroundings. He paid closer attention to sounds and soon recognized the familiar calls of juncos, nuthatches, chickadees, kinglets, a western tanager, some scrub jays, and what he thought was probably either a downy or a hairy woodpecker. Once, off in the distance, he thought he heard a flicker. A red squirrel in a tall pine started scolding him incessantly and after a while, tiring of its constant chirring, began to cut cones from the topmost branches from where they rained down all around him. When he moved on, the squirrel descended and began to gather pine seeds for winter.

Now that his ears were better attuned to the sounds around him, he took out his elk call but decided against bugling. He didn't want to draw attention to himself or startle any elk that might be close by and have it go crashing off through the brush. Instead he made several soft, plaintive cow chirps and mews. He got no response, waited a while, and tried again, with the same result. He was close enough now to the darker green patch to see that it probably was, as he had suspected, a spring or a wet area. The Basque was right, he thought. If so, he had hit pay dirt. There was plenty of grass all around and now water too. He wanted to spend a few more minutes calling before trying to approach any closer, in case there still happened to be elk within hearing. He sat down by a tree and gave several more cow calls then waited several minutes before doing it again. There was no response either time.

After a brief time he began working his way along the base of the ridge toward the green patch. As he came closer there was less and less cover. He veered higher up on the side of the canyon so that he could look down into the wet area. When he did, he saw that it was indeed a shallow marsh, larger than it first appeared, with a few areas of standing water in the rushes. And on the side closest to him there was a large wallow where the muddy ground had been freshly rutted by elk hooves. There were deep impressions where the bulls had wallowed and thrashed about and coated themselves in mud and urine. The vegetation all around the wallow was trampled and beaten down, and hanging on several bushes he saw torn strips of velvet where the bulls had been polishing their antlers.

He quickly knelt down to make himself as small and inconspicuous as possible. If he had known just how good this place was going to look he would have approached it more cautiously. It was too late for that now. His only concern at the moment was how to position and conceal himself so that he wouldn't be seen and could get a shot at any elk that approached the wallow. It was, obviously, from the looks of it, frequently in use and gave him his best chance of encountering a bull up close. He would spend the rest of the day here unless he happened to hear bugling somewhere else.

The near side of the wallow was the one most used, and the most recently too, perhaps because the ground was wetter there. The closest cover was between fifteen and twenty yards away, and five or six feet above the level of the marsh, on the side of the canyon. It consisted of a lone serviceberry bush, growing alongside the decaying trunk of a fallen tree. It was just large enough to partially screen him if he knelt down, or sat. The only better cover was twenty yards farther away. He decided he would rather be closer and take his chances on being detected than risk shooting, even at an animal as large as an elk, from as far away as forty yards. Closer is always better, he reminded himself. Why shoot from twenty yards if you can get within ten, or even five? This wasn't target archery.

He soon had made himself comfortable seated on the soft trunk of the decaying tree. He was comfortable enough that he could sit like this for a long time without having to shift his position. From his perch he could slide forward onto his left knee and shoot kneeling from beside the bush. It was, he decided, the best he was going to do.

He didn't want to bugle and call unwanted attention to himself, sitting out practically in the open like this. So for the next hour or so he gave a series of low cow calls from time to time, varying the number and the interval between them to keep it more natural and spontaneous. His attention became distracted by the sights and sounds around him and he lost track of time. At one point his foot went to sleep and he wiggled his toes and shifted ever so slightly on the log until he had restored the circulation. He became preoccupied with the chatter of a marsh wren, somewhere from within the rushes, and then the sweet, cheerful songs of several white crowned sparrows behind and above him. The cow calls elicited no response but he kept it up anyway. It gave him something to do and occupied the time. Couldn't hurt anything, he thought, so long as I don't overdo it. He judged each call on how natural it sounded and how well he thought it mimicked a cow elk. It was easy to blow a convincing bugle. The long, whistling blast was all sound and fury. A cow call was harder, subtler, and required more technique and finesse. He resisted the urge to practice and experiment with extra calls. He knew that less was better, especially if the sounds weren't perfect. He had even heard cow elk that didn't really sound to him like cow elk. There were different voices among elk, just as among the songs of birds in the same species. He couldn't imagine that the quiet calls could be heard very far, probably not even as far, he guessed, as he could see along the open meadow. But that was no reason to take a chance and become careless. Strain as he might he had not been able to hear anything at all that sounded like an elk bugling. That meant he also hadn't heard his brother bugling in the next canyon. To hear even a loud bugle very far, he imagined, you probably have to be higher up, on the ridge tops.

He gradually brought his focus in closer to his immediate surroundings. He made a mental map of the yardages to each landmark around him. He estimated that an elk standing in the edge of the wallow would be only about seventeen yards from where he was sitting. Maybe he should have paced it off in the beginning, but he hadn't wanted to take a chance on walking around out in the open. He worked his way out from there, estimating the distances to other features around him. To the other side of the wallow was about forty yards, or slightly more. Up on the opposite slope he could see what appeared to be a game trail coming from the trees up ahead and going along the far side of the marsh, and he guessed it was close to fifty yards to the closest point in the trail. The edge of the trees at the end of the meadow was about a hundred yards away, maybe more. He worked on each estimate, trying to divide the distance into smaller increments the size of which he could estimate more accurately, then adding them up to get the total. He could estimate ten yards to within a foot or so every time, and twenty yards to within a yard. But as the distances grew longer they appeared increasingly foreshortened and he had a tendency to underestimate the yardage. He worked on each estimate until he was satisfied he couldn't do any better, then memorized them. He waited a few minutes and tested himself until he could instantly recall each estimate without having to think about it. He had a mental image now of the approximate aiming picture at each distance to guide his shooting. He felt reassured that even if he missed on the first shot he wouldn't miss again, if he were lucky enough to get a second shot. He felt prepared and confident.

Then all at once he glanced to his right and there it stood, right out in the open. He could tell instantly, without even bothering to count, that there were six points on both sides. He had a catch in his breathing and his heart was suddenly racing. Where in hell did *that* come from? he wondered. It was almost as if it had materialized right out of thin air. He had heard nothing and seen nothing, no movement, not anything. But there it stood, big as you please, and no more than sixty yards away. Not an impressively large rack, he noted, but even and symmetrical. It could be the same bull he had seen earlier from up above. Perhaps his brother had pushed it over the ridge. He didn't know. The elk was moving cautiously but steadily in his direction. He's coming to the calls, he thought. He wasn't sure. But for whatever reason, it was coming through the meadow directly toward him.

As the bull neared a manzanita bush it suddenly seemed agitated and lowered its head and began thrashing the tough branches with its antlers. Its antlers were polished and free of velvet. The bull urinated in spurts on the ground and was slinging urine against itself. He could see its penis pumping back and forth in its sheath. After jousting with the bush and scratching the dirt up all around it, the elk once again moved slowly toward the wallow. Maybe he's just coming to the wallow, he thought. Whatever direction the bull took now, it was too late for him to do anything but remain still.

He had his bow resting on his lap with an arrow nocked, ready to shoot. All he had to do was slowly ease the bow up into position, and he would wait until the bull was as close as he was going to get before doing that. He'll see me for certain the moment I start drawing the bow, he told himself, so I have to be ready to shoot quickly. If the bull kept to the same path, it would pass the edge of the wallow broadside, no more than seventeen yards away. If I let him get broadside, maybe he won't see me so quickly, he thought.

For now he had to calm himself. He took a deep breath and exhaled. The bull kept coming, as if on a string. Another slow, deep breath. It appeared to be looking straight ahead. It didn't seem to take any notice of the strangely configured, camouflaged bush perched on the side of the hill. As long as I don't move, I'm all right, he thought. When I start moving though, I've got to be ready. He had no idea exactly what to expect once he began drawing his bow. Still moving cautiously, the bull was approaching the edge of the wallow. Just a few steps more and he would shoot.

As it came alongside, the bull turned its head slightly toward the wallow and away from him. Now, he thought. At the last moment he decided he would stand up to shoot. He rose slowly but steadily until he was fully upright. The bull seemed to take no notice of him. He drew his bow smoothly. Still no indication the bull saw him. When his hand reached the corner of his mouth, he released. But just as he was about to, the elk took a step down into the wallow and the arrow flashed harmlessly over its withers. He couldn't believe his eyes. He stood stunned for a moment. The elk bounded up out of the wallow, jumped forward a few yards, and halted, still partially broadside, about twenty-seven yards away, looking now over its left shoulder in his direction. He knew there was nothing to do now but keep on shooting.

He quickly stripped another arrow off the bow quiver, nocked it, aimed again behind the left shoulder, and released. At the first forward motion of the bow limbs the elk abruptly swung around hard to its right and he watched the arrow sail harmlessly past its left side, right where its shoulder had been a moment before. Now the elk took several quick steps to the right but stopped once more, this time thirty-five yards from him, angling slightly away. By then he had another arrow nocked and he shot again. He knew at once that it was too low and appeared headed beneath the elk's chest. Pick a spot! Pick a spot! he uttered under his breath. This time the elk bucked and kicked at the arrow with one hind leg and actually hit it with its hoof, shattering the brittle aluminum shaft into two pieces. The elk bounded forward a few steps and stopped again, about forty-five yards away. It was still partially broadside and he had a clear view of its right shoulder. He knew this would be the last shot he would get, and the last one he would take, no matter what. He could hardly imagine getting four shots at the same animal, standing, this close, let alone more than that.

It appeared the elk would just stand there looking back at him while he shot again. So he took his time, picked a spot behind the shoulder, and released. The arrow went to the right this time and slightly low and he saw it hit at the top of the front leg near the bottom of the chest. He heard it impact solid bone and saw that it didn't penetrate. He knew he had hit the leg and realized that it was only going to be a superficial wound, not a killing shot. The elk's right leg slightly buckled and quickly recovered. But in the next few moments the leg was suddenly sheathed in bright crimson blood, and he realized that he must have nicked the brachial artery. The elk just stood for a moment, as though slightly dazed. Then it limped forward a few steps and began slowly moving off in the direction it had come. He could not see the arrow, and knew that it had probably dislodged from the shallow wound.

What a bizarre fluke, he thought. You would never try to make that shot on purpose. It would be stupid and pointless. Even now he couldn't believe he had actually hit an artery. He didn't know his anatomy well enough to even be sure where the brachial artery was located. Perhaps it was only a vein, and the blood would clot and the bleeding stop. He sat down, emotionally drained, still keeping his eyes on the elk. It never increased its pace beyond a slow, limping walk. There was something pathetic about the sight of it, he thought. Its head was thrust forward and down and it bore the unmistakable look of defeat. He watched it finally enter the trees at the end of the meadow.

He needed time to think. He was still going over in his mind everything that had taken place since the first moment he saw the elk coming toward him. He had wanted to kill the elk cleanly. And he certainly should have. The situation was about as perfect as he could have made it. He should never have allowed himself to miss that first shot. A second sooner, or just a few moments later, and he could have made it easily. How do you end up missing an animal as large as an elk standing broadside only seventeen yards away? The next shot wasn't entirely his fault. The bull had merely thwarted him that time, but only because he had missed the easy first shot. He had simply missed the next shot on his own. And that last shot. He knew he should never have taken it. It was too far, under the circumstances, given everything that had happened. He had already had his chance and he should have just let it go at that. To finally kill it, if indeed he had, as a result of such a capricious fluke left him with the empty numbing feeling of something undeserved and dishonest. He wished now that he had just missed. Even if he killed the elk he could take no pride in it.

He walked out to the marsh to search for his arrows. He found the broken pieces of the one lying in the reeds. Two others were buried in the grass, and he did not spend any time looking for them. He would leave them as an offering to the hunting gods. He found the last arrow, lying on the ground near where the bull had been standing, the tip of the point slightly bent and the shaft coated in sticky blood. There was a clear blood trail leading off in the direction the elk had taken. It was an unmistakable artery wound. He put the bloody arrow back on his bow quiver. This one he would keep, to remind him. He could straighten the point later.

When he got to within a few yards of where he had seen the elk enter the trees, he could hear heavy, labored breathing and the low, deep, agonizing moans of suffering coming from the tall grass. The magnificent animal tried vainly once to raise its head and look toward him but collapsed again. He slowly backed away and stood listening to the dying creature's rasping death throes. He could hardly bear to listen. Even being there and witnessing it seemed an obscene and unwarranted intrusion. He did not want the dying animal to have to see him. Finally he heard one last heartrending groan, and then silence. He felt sorrowful and diminished and very bad. He could not escape the feeling of having cheated him out of his life. Maybe he was just getting old, or maybe he was finally losing his desire, or maybe he just didn't have the stomach for it anymore. But the excitement he had felt before was gone, now that the elk was dead. And in its place there was a sense of regret and shame and the loss of something intangible that could never be replaced, but also never forgotten. He didn't feel a sense of pride, only a sad guilt.

Maybe it is a different world now, he thought. Something had surely changed.

He knew he still had work to do. But it would be a bittersweet and cheerless task.

1. Is it someone, or society itself, that refuses to endorse Sam Baxter and his bank check? Why do his appeals fall on deaf ears? Is there much money likely involved? Who is the more reasonable, Mr. Ashland, Mr. Castleman, or Sam Baxter?

2. What does neat handwriting signify for Mrs. Rafferty? Why does it become so important to Andy? What does his failure signify? Why does he still want to thank her?

3. In how many ways do we see the young boy trying to insinuate himself into the world of the adults in his society? What exactly was the great bank robbery? Do you think it is something the boy could understand?

4. Is the relationship that develops between Andy and Ben Wilson one based on mutual respect, or the role of subordinate to superior? Is there any hint of shame in Andy's journey home? What specifically did Andy want to thank Ben Wilson for?

5. What were Sophie's main concerns about her world? What was the nicest surprise of all?

6. What traits and qualities does the Preacher symbolize in the story? Why is he the object of so much admiration and wonder to the crowd? What so you make of the father's comment at the end?

7. Why was it so easy for the stranger to hustle Jim Mackey? Do you think the con was planned ahead of time, or does it just unfold as a result of circumstances? Was Lola in on it all along? Was she ever really at risk?

8. What kind of cancer is Walter suffering from? What is going on between the young man and woman at the counter? What does the medical castration of Walter symbolize in the story?

9. Why was the scene between the couple on the beach so indelible to the man observing them?

10. What is the nature of the awakening in the story? Who benefits most from the experience, Andy or his father?

11. Does Andy lack confidence, or is his confidence simply of a different kind? What exactly does he mean at the end when he thinks to himself, I can live with that?

12. How does their adventure shape the young characters' confidence and concept of themselves?

13. What do we know about the characters' regard for authority? Are they being dishonest or merely trying to avoid making a bad situation worse? What can be said in defense of what they have been up to?

14. What does it mean when his brother says that it is a different world now? What has changed? Is it the world that is different, or the man?